THE MIDDLE REACHES

Cycle Two: A Rift in Time and Space

L. Andrew Cooper

Horrific Scribblings, North Hollywood, CA, USA

WARNING

The Middle Reaches is intended for a mature audience. It contains graphic violence, explicit sexuality, sexual violence, profanity, and other potentially triggering or controversial material that some readers might find unsuitable.

CONTENTS

FOREWORD

The beginning of *Cycle Two: A Rift in Time and Space* might feel like starting a sequel rather than a true continuation of the story from *Cycle One*, as it launches with an unfamiliar set of characters beginning their own Middle-Reaches-related journeys. These characters are, in fact, at a moment in time years before the opening of *Cycle One*, so *Cycle Two* might feel like a prequel... until a character familiar from *Cycle One*, operating with a temporal perspective from AFTER *Cycle One*, shows up. Time in The Middle Reaches, and in *The Middle Reaches*, doesn't work the way it should.

What should become clear, however, is that *Cycle Two*, whatever it does with timelines, comes second in the series (planned as a whole) and would make far less sense to readers who haven't read *Cycle One*. As I suggested in the previous volume's Foreword, *Cycle Two*'s major characters and conflict do come up in *Cycle One*. *Cycle Two* broadens the canvas, showing more pieces of the timeless clockwork while assuming you've got a handle on the pieces already shown.

So, I hope you enjoy spending time with Bobby, Heather, Janet, Max, Gordon, Steven, and the other characters in these pages, both unfamiliar and familiar. As for the story, the further we go, the deeper we get into the horrors of dark, dark fantasy....

L. Andrew Cooper

North Hollywood, CA, January 2025

EPISODE 16:
THE MAN IN THE
GRINNING MASK

Bobby

Bobby had to stop running. He wheezed. Steven was the runner, not him. Bobby wasn't into sports and was overweight, so he always got picked last in gym, and usually he didn't care about being out of shape, except now maybe he was going to die. The Man was chasing him. The Man in the Grinning Mask. He was real.

As Bobby struggled to catch his breath, he looked in front of him, down the hallway, long and sparkling. Familiar, too. At the beginning of the fifth grade, Mr. Burton had invited the class to talk about places they'd been, or stayed, during their summer vacations, but it was all a lead-up to Mr. Burton talking about where *he* went for his vacation, France, about which he'd prepared a long slideshow.

The coolest things about the slideshow were the pics from the Palace of Versailles, and the coolest thing about the Palace of Versailles was the Hall of Mirrors. During the summer, Bobby had read a book that talked about infinity and orders of infinity—something *way* too nerdy to share with the class—and the Hall of Mirrors made him think of it, the glass of the mirrors, the windows, the chandeliers, glass like diamonds reflecting infinities within infinities.

The burn in his lungs started to subside, and Bobby walked forward. He didn't hear anything behind him. He looked everywhere. No one else appeared to be in the hall. The glass reflected no one else.

This hallway wasn't the Hall of Mirrors at Versailles. Fifth grade was a long time ago—he was thirteen now and would start eighth grade in August—but he remembered the look of Versailles from books on castles he kept for images to use in the adventures he made up to play with Steven and Chris.

Something metallic scraped the marble floor behind him. Something sharp. With his heart in his throat, he looked back.

Nothing.

Stay calm. Stay calm.

He walked forward, his eyes everywhere, watchful for movements in the mirrors.

Unlike the one at Versailles, this hall had nothing but mirrors on both sides, each rising from the greyish floor in panels that formed an inverted U. The French Hall of Mirrors, of course, had windows on one side, which explained the light. Here the light had no explanation.

White and gold dominated the slim areas not covered with glass in the Versailles Hall of Mirrors, but here Bobby saw what seemed to be a deep red velvet, the same red as—

His cape. He's real. You have to keep running.

Bobby walked. He was faster, but he was still walking. Something moved in a mirror to his right. For a second, the movement reflected everywhere, in front of him, behind him, on both sides, infinities. Then it was gone.

He was gone.

The chandeliers were like the ones in France. They hung as triplets of elegant clusters of glass droplets supporting circles of candles, lit but not enough to explain the illumination. The paintings on the ceiling, however, were nothing like the ones at Versailles. They were not, in fact, paintings but more glass—jigsaws of stained glass formed into detailed pictures.

Instead of images of nobility and mythology, Bobby saw naked bodies, most of them human, in piles. Some of them twisted together, fingers and tongues and penises in vaginas and anuses and mouths. Every extremity entered every orifice or crevasse. Faces conveyed hunger, delight, and relish.

Other bodies, many in piles, did not express pleasure. The dismemberment of many made the continuity of corpses difficult to track. Here a woman's thigh, there a piece of a man's chest. Skin and muscle peeled away from bone. Some still living hung from walls with garlands of viscera.

Bobby tried not to look. Eyes front, steady pace, walking, not trying to run, which would only exhaust him again—

Movement in infinite reflections. Black, with a flash of red, then gone. A corner lay ahead, so a mirror stood in front of him, not very far away. He saw the movement in front of him. A reflection from behind, or maybe The Man had gotten ahead—

He kept moving, looking to his sides, looking behind him, looking ahead.

Was this Dimension X? How did he get here?

Dimension X wasn't supposed to be real, but The Man in the Grinning Mask wasn't supposed to be real, either. Bobby had made them both up, hadn't he? He used them for the fantasy game he and his friends played around the neighborhood. The Man in the Grinning Mask had been a villain for a kind of endgame. They were getting too old for make-believe.

To explain the concept of The Man to Steven, he'd had to explain spacetime as a unified idea, and he'd had to explain how there could really be more than three dimensions. Then he'd said their universe, their reality, was kind of like a cardboard box piled up with a bunch of other cardboard boxes.

They could go to Dimension X, a place where they'd been playing for years, because it was a box next to theirs, and a hole, a rift in spacetime, connected the two. The hole was in the area where Steven's street, Acton Way, dead-ended in an overgrown strip of land by Sweetwater Creek before another Acton Way began.

Bobby got close to the place where the hallway turned. Versailles had one Hall of Mirrors. Wherever he was now, there were many halls, and they were more like a mirror maze.

He'd told Steven that now all realities were in danger because The Man in the Grinning Mask, an entity who wore a black suit, a red cape, and a gold mask with a hideous grin that stretched ear to ear, was creating more rifts. He carried a long sword, and he stabbed the pile of boxes, again and again, puncturing the borders of spacetime. Time and space wouldn't work right anymore. They'd collapse.

They had to kill The Man, or The Man would kill them all.

Bobby turned the corner, and behind him, *close* behind him, he heard the squeal of metal against glass. Walking, he looked to his side—

—and saw the Grinning Mask. It looked like a comedy mask, horrific in happiness.

Bobby ran, knowing his heft would make his heart, lungs, and legs give out again soon, but when he looked to his side, he saw himself framed in a reflection with The Man he'd described to Steven, tall and thin, gold mask, black suit, red cape flowing out behind him, sword raised. The Man wore a black top hat Bobby had never seen before.

And he'd seen this Man so many times. He never told Steven that he was adding someone from his nightmares to their game. Someone from years of nightmares. Someone he might not have made up after all. Someone who had come to him. *For* him.

Someone whose sword slashed at his back. He felt the whoosh of air, but no cut.

He tried to run faster. He wished he were Steven. He wished he were good at sports. He wished he weren't such a fat slob and—

The mirrors were gone. The hallway was gone. He stumbled to a halt, mud and dead leaves at his feet. He looked behind him.

Trees. No Man. No Grinning Mask. No Hall of Mirrors.

Huge trees surrounded him, trees bigger than any he'd ever seen. He followed one's height upward into crooked, gnarled, leafless branches that intersected with other trees' dead-looking limbs, forming a canopy of shapes that looked a little like a mosaic of stained glass. The sky above, mostly occluded, was purple. Bobby couldn't be sure, but he thought the specks in it were black stars.

Heather

"You were right," Janet said. "It really is close."

Heather looked at Janet with a sideways grin. "You see? That's why it's so fucking creepy." Even on a bright, sunny day like this one, it was creepy, and that made it... thrilling.

"Did you meet anybody? From, like, the press I mean." Janet looked starry-eyed when she said, "the press." She was the only person Heather knew who could get excited by local newspeople.

"No," Heather said. "They were mostly done with the story by the time I got here from my mom's." She and Janet stood at the curb on Acton Way, looking down the slope of the Marks house's driveway. "I did meet a cop, though."

"What was he like?"

"Young," Heather said, looking at the house instead of Janet. "And cute. The cops still come around here, you know."

"How young was he?"

Heather blushed and laughed. "You know, I *did* ask. Twenty-four."

Janet looked scandalized. "That's not young!"

"You get a different perspective in college," Heather said. Heather was nineteen. Janet was a young seventeen, about to start her senior year in high school. They'd been friends forever, since Heather's parents had still been married and had played bridge with Janet's parents, and the age difference had never mattered that much.

"I guess so," Janet said. "We're here for psychokiller stuff, right? We totally failed the Bechdel Test."

"We would have failed anyway," Heather said. "The psychos were boys." She started walking down the driveway.

Janet followed her. "Do you think we can get inside?"

The "KEEP OUT by Order of County Sheriff" sign on the front door was clearly visible. "I wouldn't want my DNA in there. Like I said, cops still come around, and they're still looking for those boys, Gordon and Steven Marks, so they'd follow up on any new... leads." As she spoke, Heather led them into the yard, toward the left side of the house.

"Where are we going?" Janet asked. She had short brown hair, fair skin, big green eyes, and pink lips. She wore an orange-and-white-striped shirt that didn't cover her belly button and high-cut denim shorts that hugged her narrow hips. She was cute, turning into a pretty young woman but not a beauty.

"We might get a peek. I think one of the basement rooms has windows," Heather said. She knew the crucial room had windows because she had read about it on the internet, but she hadn't come to check because she'd preferred to wait for company.

They got to the backyard gate, and Heather opened it. She was already through when Janet said, "Are you sure we're not trespassing?"

"We're trespassing," Heather said, "but the police only put signs on the house itself, and the owners aren't here to mind." She figured Janet would let the rationalization pass.

Janet followed her through the gate. "By 'the owners' you mean the parents, right? I never heard what happened to them."

They walked through overgrown grass past the house's side, which, as the slope continued downward, revealed a basement with partial windows. Heather knew where she was going, though, and kept going while she said, "Calvin Marks went into a kind of fugue state or something when he found out what his sons had done. Jessica Marks apparently... just... took off. Disappeared. Not unlike her boys."

They passed the corner, the fence within a fence, a pool area, which they entered so that Heather could lead them to the full window of the basement's back room, the room where the murders had happened.

"You seem to know a lot," Janet said. "You seem to know where you're going. What got you so interested, I mean, other than spending half the summer with your dad right nearby in Rolling Vistas?"

Using her hands to shield the sides of her face from sunlight, Heather brought her face as close as she could to a windowpane. The effort yielded a view of the room, fake wood panels on the walls, cheap green carpet... and nothing. Not the folding lawn chair the girl had been raped and murdered on, not an outline of where the boy's body had been found mutilated—

Except maybe that dark spot *was* a bloodstain. It might have been a shadow.

Janet stood on her right, shielding her eyes like Heather did, peering inside. "What am I supposed to see?"

Heather turned away from the window, sighed, and said, "It's been too long. They probably got whatever evidence they needed, took the good stuff away, and basically cleaned up."

She exited the pool area and wandered further into the backyard, where it leveled off as it neared the creek. Janet followed. Heather stared at the creek as she said, "You asked me why I'm so interested. It's because this kid I used to babysit, Bobby Lightfoot, disappeared a few months before the murders in this house, and people generally assume that Gordon Marks killed him. But I don't know."

Janet looked at the creek, too. "What don't you know?"

Across the creek, contained by the Markses' fence, a dense area of trees and brush looked like a sample of the woods at the end of Acton Way. Bobby had talked about it. He, Steven Marks, and the boy killed in the basement—Chris Ledbetter—had played back there. It was a place for their fantasy adventures. They had a lot of fantasy adventures.

The girl the Marks boys murdered in the basement was Chris's older sister, Annie. She'd been a little younger than Janet.

"I don't know who all Gordon and Steven killed, but Bobby... I have a feeling," Heather said.

Janet kept staring at the creek. Did she hear it? Hear that it was too narrow to be so loud? Its babbles were whispers. Heather thought she heard her own name, but she wouldn't have sworn to anything.

Janet said, "What kind of feeling?"

"It's stupid," Heather said, turning toward Janet.

Janet faced her, and Heather became aware of how exposed they were, standing in the backyard of the abandoned murder house, where anyone could see them. Janet said, "I doubt it's stupid. Stupid isn't particularly you."

"First of all," Heather said, leading with the rational argument, "Bobby and Steven were, like, best friends. I don't think Steven would have. I don't know about Gordon, but at least for Steven, Bobby would have been on the safe list." Bobby Lightfoot, but not Chris Ledbetter. *Marginally* rational. "Second of all," Heather said, and she paused before continuing: "and this is the weird part."

"It's all pretty weird," Janet said.

"Bobby had a kind of... boogeyman," Heather said. "When I was babysitting, and his parents stayed out late, he would get up at night, upset, and he told me about him. He called him The Man in the Grinning Mask."

"Grinning... Mask?"

"It's gold. It reminds me of a comedy mask, from the classic comedy and tragedy pair? You can't see anything behind it, no eyes, no mouth, even though the mouth on the mask is spread wide, stretching from ear to ear in a way that's kind of unnatural." The image wavered in Heather's mind. "He's tall and skinny, and he wears a black suit with a long red cape. He carries a sword. Sometimes it has blood on it."

"You sound like you've seen him," Janet said. Her face had gotten paler, as if *she* had seen a ghost.

"I have," Heather said. "After Bobby told me about him, I dreamed about him, too. Only, my dreams add a black top hat. A magician's hat. He reaches down toward his feet and pulls rabbits out of nowhere. He stuffs the rabbits in his hat, and they disappear. A magic trick, but backward. For some reason, it scares the hell out of me. *He* scares the hell out of me."

"He sounds scary." Silence. They looked at each other until Janet continued, "You think Bobby got stuffed in the hat, don't you?"

Heather shook her head. "Not literally, but... *something*

happened to make him disappear. Something nobody understands. Not yet." Another silence. "I told you it was stupid."

Janet looked back toward the window into the room where the Marks boys had slaughtered the Ledbetter kids. "Standing right here, a lot of freaky shit sounds easier to believe."

Gordon

They'd cleaned up, changed clothes, and left the house long before their parents got home and before anyone thought of looking for Annie or Chris. Gordon's idea had been to go to the Mortimers, who would know what to do. He would bring Steven, who had surprised him by beating Annie to death with a baseball bat once Gordon was done with her. Maybe watching Chris die had broken him.

They really were brothers now.

Steven had come close to meeting Adam before, when Steven and Chris had gone snooping at the Mortimers' house, right at the beginning of the other Acton Way, and Adam had chased them back to the creek in the middle. Gordon had intervened, and the younger boys had gotten away. Adam might not like seeing Steven again, but Gordon would make him understand why he was proud of the little guy.

Gordon, age fifteen, looked at Steven, age twelve, and felt a bond with him for the first time. Before, Steven had been in the way. He'd hung on when he should have disappeared. Now he was something... else.

The Mortimers might not have been happy to see either of them. Adam and Ellie had rules, the big one being NIMBY, which stood for Not In My Back Yard. Go hunting near where you sleep, and you get caught. Annie, Chris, and the others broke the NIMBY rule big time. Adam and Ellie might have thought

Gordon and Steven had become... too risky.

Gordon didn't get a chance to find out what the adult pair thought of his and his brothers' recent activities because, when they entered the Mortimers' house through the back door, which led into the kitchen, they found no one in the house, only a note on the kitchen table that said, "Follow the creek."

Gordon didn't know what the note meant, but Steven had a pretty good idea, so, a minute later, they were back outside in the humidity, under the bright blue summer sky, walking toward the area between the two Acton Ways, the clearing and the place where Sweetwater Creek got so much bigger than it was behind their house.

Steven led them along by the creek side, saying something about "Dimension X." He was probably talking about his game with Bobby and Chris. Gordon knew they came down here for their baby-shit make-believe. The place was too muddy and thorny to interest the older kids, who preferred Cooper's Pond in nearby Rolling Vistas for make-out sessions and... whatever, but Steven and his faggy friends liked it.

Steven didn't have friends anymore.

The funniest thing happened. They walked along, the sky faded from blue to white, and strange noises—buzzing insects, cawing birds, hints of voices, all with unfamiliar fierceness— surrounded them. Then everything went black.

Vision returned, and they still stood by the creek, but it looked different. Deeper, maybe. And it was red, reflecting the sky, which was also red, and in it were streaks of pink and purple, and bruises, bruises that might have been shaping up into circles.

The noises had intensified, adding layers of screeching, and shrieking, and—voices Gordon could understand. Steven looked confused. Gordon wasn't.

Steven said, "Where...?"

"We skipped ahead," Gordon said. "We're in the same place, but further along."

"How...?"

Gordon didn't know how, but he kept them moving, and they blacked out again, and again, finding themselves under a pink sky, or a purple, or a white, or back under a red, the line of the creek jumbled, but they always moved along the same trajectory, following the creek. The more they skipped, the more Gordon understood.

This place was helping them search, not just for Adam and Ellie, but for others. This place wasn't called Dimension X. It was called The Middle Reaches, and it was a hunting ground.

Janet

In the waning summer evening sunlight, Janet drove through the narrow two-lane roads of Rolling Vistas, having left Heather to a night of new releases and popcorn with her dad. Mr. Park had always seemed more comfortable treating Heather like a friend rather than a daughter, but since Heather was so independent, the lack of parenting seemed okay.

Janet admired Heather's independence. Janet would have liked her dad to treat her like a daughter or a friend. Like something, anyway.

Janet admired a lot about Heather. Heather had gotten into Columbia University, for God's sake, and had spent most of the last year in *New York City*. Janet planned to apply to schools in New York. NYU, maybe. She'd have to write a damned good application. Her grades were not quite up to Heather's standards.

Heather—with perfect, smooth golden skin, long black hair, deep black eyes, and curves that called out to be touched— set a standard for beauty that Janet couldn't reach, either.

Rolling Vistas connected to Acton Way, which wasn't

technically part of any neighborhood as far as Janet could tell, a short distance before the "Dead End" sign. She turned away from the sign, toward the Marks house, where she stopped and idled in front of the driveway's steep downward slope. Except for the KEEP OUT sign on the black front door, the big yellow house looked innocuous.

Kids murdering kids in the suburbs. It was a great topic. Heather seemed drawn to the sensational aspect, as well as her personal connection. Janet's angle was the American Tragedy. What stains did the atrocities committed by the Marks boys leave on the surrounding neighborhoods and the kids in them who were trying to grow up and live normal lives?

She'd be spending time with Heather anyway, so Heather would be her lens. Heather's reaction to the murders, her fascination—her interest in Bobby Lightfoot's disappearance—whatever steps she would take to find out more. Janet would follow her. Study her. Write about her. The long version of her essay on this American Tragedy might even be publishable.

And the short version? A damned good application.

EPISODE 17: WHAT HAPPENED TO BOBBY LIGHTFOOT?

Bobby

Bobby Lightfoot had fallen into a rift in time and space.

Maybe he was *still* falling.

Standing among these giant trees, gnarled branches like skeleton hands, the smell of honeysuckle and death consuming him, he tried to work backwards, to connect this place with a life he would recognize.

He'd been a kid. Middle school. Reading and studying physics and math on a college level, but he didn't spread that information around too much. He'd tried to be a normal kid and succeeded, well enough.

He didn't feel like a kid anymore.

Stepping backward from where he stood now, under this strange purple sky, toward being that kid, he landed in the mirror maze, getting chased by The Man in the Grinning Mask. Dimension X? If The Man was real, making rifts in spacetime with his sword, Bobby might be in a reality he'd never conceived, or sliding through realities—

But that was make-believe.

It felt more like make-believe because before he'd been

running through the halls of mirrors, he'd been lying in the clearing between the two Acton Ways, the place where he, Steven, and Chris pretended to pass through the portal into Dimension X. He lay in the dirt, confused, unhurt, alone, and certain something very bad had happened to him.

Gordon Marks. Gordon said Steven and Chris were waiting for him. Bobby knew better than to trust Gordon, but Gordon was convincing, and Bobby couldn't let Gordon tell the others Bobby had refused to come see them for whatever serious talk was supposed to happen. Bobby had to know, to be sure. He followed Gordon to the dead end, into the clearing. He let Gordon trick him.

Bobby touched his lips. Gordon had put tape over his mouth. He'd tried to scream through the tape, knowing it wouldn't do any good. In some situations, being a genius doesn't help. When you're terrified, being a genius doesn't help.

Gordon made him take off his clothes. When he woke up, lying in the dirt, alone—Gordon was gone—he had his clothes on. But he remembered how exposed he'd felt. Embarrassed. He hated changing in the locker room. At least in clothes he didn't think as much about other people seeing his body.

The knife. When, at first, Bobby refused to undress, Gordon cut his shirt with that big knife. When he woke up later, the shirt wasn't cut anymore.

Gordon tied him to a tree and called him ugly. He felt ugly. He was ugly.

What happened next felt like a knot in Bobby's brain. He heard sounds of a shovel piercing the earth, of dirt falling on dirt. He felt agony, hard hits against his legs, his sides, his arms, his stomach, his chest, blood where his back scraped against the tree. Parts of him broke. He heard his bones break.

The knife cut him. Between his thighs. Gordon cut it off.

When he woke up between the two Acton Ways, his body

was whole. No broken bones. Nothing missing. What happened with Gordon felt like a dream.

He sat up, got to his knees, then to his feet, brushing off dirt as he tried to orient himself. The day was hot—this morning had been cold. *Was it even the same day?*

An odd thought, but everything felt different. *He* felt different. Had what happened with Gordon... happened?

Insistent babbling drew him toward the creek. Despite the current, the surface was clear enough to show him a reflection. He gazed at the reflection, dizzy. The boy he saw was not himself.

The boy the creek reflected was older, fit, handsome. His hair was lighter than Bobby's, and his skin was paler. The reflection was good enough for Bobby to make out the boy's icy blue eyes. The boy wore a blue-and-white striped polo t-shirt. They smiled at each other, and Bobby thought the person in the reflection looked young, but he didn't look like a kid.

After seeing that reflection, Bobby found himself in the mirror maze.

Later, standing among the giant trees with the purple sky above him, Bobby thought about not being a kid anymore. The kid he remembered was dead. He was something else now.

Max

Max woke up with a hollow feeling in his stomach. It wasn't hunger. He felt on top of and then underneath his black t-shirt because the feeling was more like someone had scooped out his insides, but his midsection felt okay. Too warm, maybe. Black shirt, black jeans, and the summer sun in a blue sky overhead—he'd probably start sweating soon.

He lay in the dirt. Where the hell was he? The trees, the bushes, the briars, the scent of honeysuckle—the babbling of the creek nearby—he knew where he was. He was in the area between the two unconnected streets called Acton Way.

Why was he here, lying in the dirt? How did he get here? So, this area was between two streets called Acton Way, but where was that, exactly? Did he live nearby? He didn't know where he lived! Wait—

Who was he?

He had a name. Max.

"See you later, Max."

Who had said that? In a context he couldn't remember, it portended ill. Like the feeling in his stomach. The scooped-out feeling.

Like his brain. Scooped out.

Other than a name and a location, both of which needed context, he could have told you things he sensed about himself. He was a reasonably intelligent teenager. Despite gloomy interests, he didn't get into anything more rebellious than smoking pot occasionally. He was a good kid who liked girls and books, in that order. He didn't seem to lack personality, only personhood.

Assuming he wasn't an orphan, who and where were his parents? Did he have siblings? Pets? He probably went to school —when it wasn't summer, and he was sure it was summer— but he didn't know where. He didn't remember getting dressed this morning. Or eating, but he must have done so, or he'd have hunger in addition to the scooped sensation. Presumably.

Why did he have a paralyzing sense of dread? Like someone had *put him in* this situation? More than that, he felt like, when he stood up from where he inexplicably lay, he would set events into motion that he would rather not encourage. He would rather not, but he would, because—

because he had no choice—

because he had a *purpose*—

because his name was Max, and he began in the space between the two Acton ways, and he had a purpose to serve.

That something awful might have happened to him was, at least for the moment, irrelevant. He would ignore the sensation in his stomach. He stood and looked across the creek, not toward—

(The Middle Reaches)

the direction of the current, but toward the street. He would go there first. He needed to meet a girl, a young woman, named Heather. Even though the vaguest sense of his own home eluded him, the way to her house came to him as easily as his name. He needed to meet her. He would be charming. He had information to share, information she had to believe.

He needed to tell her about Bobby Lightfoot. He didn't know what he would tell her. That would come to him later.

He walked toward Rolling Vistas. He had a purpose to serve.

Heather

"It's like an old-fashioned sleepover. We can watch horror movies and scare the shit out of ourselves." To facilitate the retro atmosphere, Heather dug her comfiest set of cotton pajamas out of the dresser. *She* certainly wouldn't be shy about answering the door for the pizza guy in her PJs.

"I thought the whole point," Janet said, "was *not* to be scared."

"Want to borrow some PJs?" Heather asked.

Janet hopped off the bed and fetched her overnight bag from the spot by the door. "Got my own." She wasn't questioning the decision to change into nightclothes before sundown.

Heather pulled off her shirt and, after a moment's hesitation, took off her bra. She felt Janet's eyes on her. Heather's tits weren't huge but were bigger than Janet's. Janet's gaze didn't feel envious, exactly. As she finished changing into her pajama top, Heather said, "You're here so that being scared doesn't matter. I didn't want to be alone while my dad's out of town, but having you here makes it better."

"I feel that way, too," Janet said.

"What way?"

"Oh, um," and Janet changed into her pajama bottoms, shorts in a silk set much sexier than what Heather had chosen, "you know, being scared isn't as scary when you're not alone."

"Completely," Heather said, and she sighed. She sat on the bed, and when she finished changing, Janet sat next to her. "Besides, I think watching Michael Myers go after Laurie Strode would provide some relief in a weird way. Because that shit's not real. But it *really happened* here. At that house I showed you. In this neighborhood. And it's messing with my head."

"I don't blame you," Janet said. "I keep thinking about it, too. I've read about it some."

"Yeah, and it's like, those Marks boys, Gordon and Steven, are younger than both of us. I can't imagine ever... but being that young, and... having what it takes to...." Heather shuddered, but it felt unnatural.

"I know," Janet said.

"Did you...." Heather blushed. "This is an awkward question."

"I'm up for awkward questions," Janet said.

"Well, I know you're into journalism and all," Heather said. "Did you ever go back and watch any of those videos that ended up online, the political ones, like the execution of Saddam Hussein, or of Daniel Pearl, or something like that?"

Janet blushed. "Why? Did you?"

"I don't suppose I'd be asking if I didn't peek," Heather said.

"Well, yeah," Janet said. "Who isn't curious, right?"

Heather nodded and paused. She wasn't drunk. Her first year of college had taught her that saying this sort of thing was easier when drunk. "This is kind of crazy, but I've been thinking... if someone had shot a video of what Gordon and Steven Marks did, I would... I would really like to see it."

For an instant, Heather thought she saw disgust flash across Janet's face, but a look of understanding replaced it so quickly that she couldn't be sure. "Like I said," and Janet inhaled, "who isn't curious?"

"Right," Heather said. She stood, walked toward the closet, and spun to face Janet. "It's like I need evidence to believe, completely. Which is my problem with what did or didn't happen to Bobby Lightfoot. I'm not convinced Gordon did it, so I need more. Proof of something."

"I imagine his parents feel the same way," Janet said.

"Yeah, well, they're not doing anything. What if there were a way to... to learn more? To find out, for certain, what really happened to Bobby Lightfoot?"

Janet

The air conditioner must have been set in the low 60s, too cold for Janet in her pajamas, but she wouldn't complain. She followed Heather to the kitchen, where Heather offered her a bottle and corkscrew. "It's a Malbec," Heather said, "from Argentina. Dad said he didn't mind if I got into the wine, as long as I didn't tell Mom."

Janet didn't know anything about Malbec, but having done so for her parents even though she wasn't allowed to drink, she knew how to cork a bottle of wine, so she did. She handed the bottle back to Heather, who had two glasses ready. "What were you saying," Janet said, "about learning more? Finding out what really happened?"

"I don't know," Heather said, pouring. "I was what if-ing."

"Were you thinking about doing some kind of investigation?" The idea of Heather playing Nancy Drew made Janet's heart beat a little faster. Not that she'd ever read any books about Nancy Drew, or even had a clear sense of what kind of person Nancy Drew was. But Heather Park, detective —alongside Janet Fillion, investigative journalist—conjured alluring possibilities. Heather, in charge. Alluring.

"Maybe," Heather said, handing over a full glass of red wine. "I wouldn't know where to start."

Janet took a big sip of the wine and let it slide over her tongue. She knew wine was supposed to taste like other things and thought she tasted plums. Maybe mentioning it to Heather would impress her—but maybe she should stay on topic. "There was that cop."

"What cop?" Heather said, sipping.

"The one you said you met. The twenty-four-year-old guy..."

"Oh," Heather said with a smile. "Stu. Greenfield. Officer Greenfield. Yeah." Heather swirled the wine in her glass. "I don't suppose he'd answer if I called 911, but I could track him down." She smiled. "He *was* cute. I could ask him out."

Janet forced a sly laugh.

"I don't think he'd know anything, though," Heather continued. "The cops don't know anything about Bobby. The kid simply disappeared, no trace, months before the Marks boys offed their neighbors. Any connection is speculation."

Janet started, "Because they never found—" but she

stopped herself. *Bobby's body*. It sounded silly in her head. *Bobby's body*. Silly and serious at the same time. Were they trivializing the probable death of a child? Of children? *Offed their neighbors*. That word, "offed." Heather sounded so above it all, and Janet liked the way she sounded, and she didn't know if she should. Janet sipped Malbec.

At least the detachment, the *alienation*, would make a good point in her essay.

"No, they never found him," Heather said. "His body, I mean, assuming he's dead."

In Janet's head, she and Heather walked into a room of old men gathered around a table. The men made room for them. On the table was the naked body of a boy, his chest and middle cut open, heart, lungs, liver, stomach, and intestines gleaming. Janet had a camera and a notepad. She would record, and Heather would examine. They would find clues. Bobby's body would tell them a story.

It was gruesome. It was... morbid. The only thing that stopped her from looking at the corpse in her mind was looking at Heather, standing only a few feet away. Janet drank Malbec.

"Oh shit," Heather said.

"What?"

"We forgot to make a toast!" Heather grabbed the wine bottle and motioned for Janet to offer her glass. Janet did, and Heather gave each of them a top-off before getting into clinking position, their hands close, their faces close. "To what shall we toast?"

Janet thought as she tried to keep her breathing steady. "To... making new discoveries." She held her breath, sinking into Heather's deep, dark eyes. "Together."

"Together," Heather said. They clinked glasses, drank, and smiled at each other, faces still close.

Janet leaned forward and kissed Heather softly on the mouth. Heather pulled back. With a polite giggle, Heather said, "Save it for the next Stu Greenfield who comes along. We're not kids anymore."

Janet forced another laugh, stepped back, and drank. "Isn't it a little cold in here?"

"Come on," Heather said, walking toward the doorway. "There's a blanket on the living room sofa. You get comfy, and I'll pull out my dad's movie collection."

Heather

Bobby was a pudgy white boy with brown hair and too many chins, but he was still a little kid, not too much older than when Heather had stopped babysitting, but with a fragile —it had to be innocence—despite knowing too much about way too many things. She didn't know where he was, but she saw him looking like he must have looked around the time when he... disappeared.

He was lost. Enormous trees, so tall and so big around that Heather couldn't guess where they were, surrounded him. Knobby roots stuck out of the ground, and twisted branches arched through the sky, which was... wrong. Purple, dotted with black. Shimmering black. Like black stars.

Not all the naked branches were high above him as he trod over roots and dead leaves, navigating through the trees without any direction. Some branches came close to him. Some brushed by his sides. He mostly seemed to ignore them. He ignored them, Heather thought, because he had too much to monitor—the ground at his feet, a way ahead, openings in the trees to his sides and behind him.

So many sources of danger. The noises, the insects, the birds, the shrieking of incoherent voices that might or might not have been human—they all threatened. And *he* could be here.

The Man in the Grinning Mask.

Footsteps among twigs and nettle, footsteps surer than his own. The Man in the Grinning Mask wore black boots with high heels that clicked on marble and pounded on dirt. Within the trees behind Bobby—a flash of the red cape? A glint of the shadowy woods' dim light off the bright golden mask?

Heather called out, "Bobby! Bobby, I'm here! You're not alone!" *You're not alone.* Was that a comfort or a warning? Reassuring or terrifying? Would he even recognize her voice? "It's me, Heather Park!"

Bobby stopped walking and looked over his shoulder as if he had heard something. Heather didn't feel like he looked in her direction. Heather didn't feel like she *had* a direction. She wasn't with him, not physically. She slept in her bed at her father's house. This experience was—

A dream? A vision? She didn't believe in visions. But she felt like Bobby was in trouble, and she wanted to protect him. He was lost in—she needed to find him in—

(The Middle Reaches)

—the place that had taken him. The place where The Man was close. The place where branches reached out and scratched his skin as he walked forward again. As he moved faster, the branches grabbed at him. When he tried to run, they caught him, more and more twisting, circling extensions of naked, dead-looking but animated wood, ensnaring him. He couldn't move.

They pulled on his legs. They pulled on his arms. They pulled harder. Harder. Bobby opened his mouth to scream.

He made no sound. Desperation quaked in his eyes and around his lips. The branches tore his limbs from their sockets. Blood flowed.

Heather screamed. She screamed for the boy. She screamed for herself.

She sat up in bed, breath heavy, tears on her cheeks. Janet lay beside her, curled up with her back to her. "Janet," she whispered. "Janet, are you awake?"

No response.

Heather lay back down, turned toward Janet, and scooted until their bodies were close. Seeking warmth, seeking comfort, she wrapped an arm around her friend's shoulders.

A few seconds later, one of Janet's hands squeezed Heather's arm. Acceptance. Heather couldn't trust herself to go back to sleep, but she felt better.

Sheldon

He waited. He knew better than to wonder *how long* he'd been waiting, or would be waiting, because lengths of time meant nothing here. Nick and Leslie had looked older, significantly older, but he might have been older than they were, might have been sitting here, in the Cavern of The Mouth, for a century. Or a week. No sense speculating.

For what felt like a long time, he'd thought he was waiting for Nick. The promise would be fulfilled, at last, and he would be free to move along. To go through the Gate. To see the other side. But The Watcher had wanted Nick for a purpose Sheldon now understood, at least mostly. And The Middle Reaches themselves, through him, had... reassigned... Leslie.

Somebody new had entered the path, and Sheldon had a role to play. He would know more when... time... and space... aligned... or did whatever they had to do. He would wait until then. Sitting in his underwear in this place where water dripped without end, where he should have felt cold but didn't. That was his purpose, for now. But his purpose would grow.

Another storyteller was coming. They would make a new story together.

EPISODE 18: TRAPPED IN THE RIFT

Steven

Steven still felt afraid of Gordon, who didn't seem afraid of this... place... where they were, and of the way they blipped in and out like someone was flipping light switches in their brains, with each new "on" landing them in a different... section... pink sky or red sky or purple sky, two moons above or no moon at all. Were they in Dimension X? Or The Dark Place, about which Bobby had only given him hints?

Gordon called it "The Middle Reaches." How did he know? The whispers, always whispers, whispers Steven couldn't understand.

Were they in Hell?

Steven didn't understand what he'd done. He'd killed Annie Ledbetter. He got that. He didn't understand why he'd done it, though it felt right, in a way, and Gordon seemed proud. He was supposed to hate Gordon, but he didn't. They'd fought all their lives. Their parents usually ignored it as "sibling rivalry," but Steven always knew it was more than that. Sometimes, Gordon wanted to kill him.

Except he didn't now. Which was good, because they couldn't go home. They didn't have parents. They had each other.

Gordon thought they might find the Mortimers, Adam

and Ellie, his friends—except maybe not his friends, because he said something about them not approving of what Steven and Gordon had done. Steven had seen Adam. Adam scared the shit out of him.

Under a red sky, streaked with pink and purple, they walked on narrow land between a row of tall trees and the creek. Wherever they were, whatever surrounded them, they walked as if they had a place to go, and they looked around as if they had something, or someone, to find.

Gordon held out his hand. "Stop," he said. "Look at that."

He gestured toward trees a short distance ahead of them. "What?" Steven said.

"Between those trees," Gordon said. "The web."

Squinting and stepping closer, Steven began to see thin filaments, silvery-red, inset polygons on rays attached to diseased bark and branches, a spiderweb, taller than he was, wider than his arm-span, easy to miss until his eyes caught the intricate threads, then brilliant to see in its imprisoning architecture.

In a high corner, higher than his head, crouched the spider, bigger than a cat, with a brown, furry, sectioned body, long, bent-knuckled legs, and a head—

bald—

white-skinned—

brown-eyed—

human.

Steven's mind flashed to the movie *The Fly*, not the really gross one but the old one with Vincent Price, where the fly with the human head screams, "Help me, help me!" This spider wouldn't ask for help. Its mouth bulged with fangs. Its bulbous eyes had vertical slits for pupils. It waited. It hunted.

Steven and Gordon were hunters. Gordon said so.

The constant caws blended with the other sounds of this place, and Steven didn't think much of them or the fluttering within the trees, but when a black bird—wings tattered like a flag in a firefight—burst from a branch and swooped near the web, he and Gordon both watched.

The spider-man—Spiderman!—raised its body and shot webbing that snared the bird and pulled it into the web, where it stuck. A natural spider, Steven thought, would finish the job by bundling the bird into a kind of cocoon.

The spider with the humanoid head rushed to the trapped bird and sunk in its fangs. The bird made a weak noise but seemed to die quickly.

Gordon laughed. Like everything else, he took the unnatural display in stride. "I wish I could build a web," Gordon said.

Gordon was good at building things. His bedroom was full of the model airplanes he'd been putting together for years. Steven wasn't thinking about them being the web-builders, though. He thought about the bird. Stuck, like he was. Trapped in a rift in spacetime, like Bobby talked about.

"I'd build a web and catch people," Gordon said. "Like our basement. Our basement could have been a web."

Maybe Gordon was partly right. Maybe they were spiders, but this place wasn't their web. They were unnatural creatures visiting the web of another, far greater creature, and sooner or later, it would want something from them. That scared Steven most of all.

Bobby

The more Bobby tried to find his way through the trees, the more endless the trees seemed. He fought back panic, the desire to run even though he had no direction and no energy left

—the trees towered, menaced, and he felt small. Small and dizzy. Trees circled him, rocked back and forth, threatened to spin.

Along with the caws, the screeches, the roars, the shrieks, the screams, Bobby heard, closer, rustling in the dead leaves and nettle, snapping twigs, signals of movement in the circling trees. The trees themselves, dark among shadows, didn't always look like trees. Sometimes they had shoulders. Shoulders and long bodies and arms that reached. Sometimes they were assassins, hunched with knives, running in circles around him. Bobby's vision blurred.

A new sound joined the others. Growls, like the low rumbles of trucks. Woof! Woof! Woof! Woof!

Dogs but... bigger. Wolves? Maybe.

Assassins circled. Bobby slipped between them, advancing, unsure whether he maintained a consistent course, guessing he didn't, wondering whether he should, because no matter which way he went—

WOOF. WOOF.

They got closer.

He couldn't think about that. The... assassins... circled... with knives. Trees with low, pointy branches, curled fingers, grasped. Everything blurred. His feet scuffed against uneven ground, making him teeter as he stepped, stepped, stepped forward, between two assassins, avoiding knives, into a new space, new circles, assassin trees, WOOF! But he had to keep standing, because if he fell—

Ahead, the light changed. Bobby aimed for ahead. Birds fluttered over him, showing talons. Assassins, so hard to see clearly, reached for him with knives.

Emerging from the trees, Bobby stopped because the circles stopped. Trees, or assassins, or whatever they were, no longer encircled him, but ahead, like some nightmare of knitting, a mesh of vines, some bigger than Bobby's legs, formed a low wall that extended left and right as far as he could see. The vines, most of them thorny, *moved*.

Or was the way they slithered around each other an effect of Bobby's distorted vision?

Another new sound. Bobby heard water rushing behind the vines.

Bobby looked toward the sky, easier to see without the skeletal canopy of branches. Purple, black stars, two bluish-grey moons... his eyes cleared. His thoughts cleared. He was in a definite place. It was not a place he had invented, not Dimension X, but it wasn't a normal place, either. Thinking of it as a rift in spacetime felt apt enough. Bobby did not prefer purely supernatural explanations.

When he looked back at the wall of vines, the thorny threads' movements changed. They pulsed and spread apart. Most of them, from the top to about a foot from the ground, bumped upward as they pulsed, while those at the bottom stretched outward and downward. Bobby's eyes stuck on the length of some of the thorns—more knives—before he realized what had formed in front of him.

A passage.

The vines had made an opening, thorns at the top, thorns to step over, big enough for Bobby to fit through. Could Bobby trust...?

Something rustled in the trees behind him. He stepped through the opening and hurried away, looking over his shoulder as he put distance between himself and the animated thorny threads that tightened together, knitted shut, before he managed many steps.

The rushing water turned his attention, and he saw the creek. He didn't know how, but he *knew* it was Sweetwater Creek, or a version of it, which ran behind Steven's house, and got bigger between the two Acton Ways, where they pretended to enter Dimension X, but this place still couldn't be Dimension X, because Sweetwater Creek was different—

and Bobby was different.

Woof-woof-woof-woof-woof-woof-woof!

Bobby looked upstream and saw them, two of them, approaching along the shore. Like German Shepherds, only much larger, and *yellow*, radiant yellow, with too many legs, and mouths too wide for their heads, like clowns' smiles—almost like grinning masks—with lolling jaws showing teeth, too many teeth like in sharks' mouths.

One of them snarled, viscous drool coursing from its too-red tongue, which matched its piercing eyes.

If Bobby tried to run, they'd catch him. He stood paralyzed.

Sheldon

He finished dressing, pulling on the blue and white striped polo that he supposed was the only shirt he would ever wear again. Strange that he didn't have shoes. He didn't worry about hurting his feet, but he still felt like he ought to have shoes. What if the newcomer noticed? Being barefoot in terrain like The Middle Reaches was tantamount to wearing a toe-tag.

Or maybe that was Sheldon's new-found cynicism. Maybe the new one, Bobby, wouldn't come to dark conclusions based on a lack of tennis shoes. Or maybe he had already figured things out and had made peace. Maybe Bobby Lightfoot was Zen. Precociously Enlightened, and about to be folded under Sheldon's wing.

At least he assumed that was the plan. The Cavern talked to him. If it didn't, he'd certainly go mad with boredom, but it talked in layers, multiple messages at once, sometimes in loops. Sometimes the messages weren't in a language he recognized, but he could intuit meanings. He couldn't differentiate between noises outside, mingling with the dripping water, and inside his head. He didn't care.

What might have been days ago, the chatter on several layers had changed and converged on a theme, a theme of Sheldon leaving the Cavern and going to meet Bobby Lightfoot. He would help the younger boy, serve as a guide.

Serve. Sheldon's purpose was to serve. He had served Nick and Leslie, hadn't he? All the while serving—

Guide. These, young friend, are The Middle Reaches, where many transition from bold and living to... less so... but not you. I am here to ensure your safe passage to the Gate. What happens there, however—

Sheldon had a strong suspicion about what would happen there. Young Master Lightfoot was special. Young Master Lightfoot would not be reassigned to serve on the earthly side of the Gate. He would pass through. Sheldon would facilitate.

And whether *the one he served* intended it or not, he would join his charge in reaching the other side.

What, or whom, did he serve? At the average moment, he thought he served The Middle Reaches. But when he contemplated his service specifically, he knew that The Middle Reaches was the domain of one of the old gods on the other side of the Gate. He had told the story to Nick, Leslie, Celia, Ambrose, and Pedro. Might he serve the God of the Palace, Hastur, the King in Yellow?

He needed answers, and he might need this... Bobby Lightfoot... to bring him to the answers. So, he would serve, obediently, and give the boy whatever he needed. He would make the boy love him.

And so, he would venture out of the Cavern for the first time in what felt like millennia.

Heather

Heather cracked two eggs in one hand, then spilled their innards with the others in the mixing bowl and started beating them with a fork. She had the fan on to vent the smoke from the sizzling bacon, and Janet sat on the other side of room, at the kitchen table reading news on Heather's computer, so Heather had to project her voice. "I had a pretty freaky dream last night."

"Maybe we shouldn't have gotten into your dad's Japanese horror collection," Janet said.

"I don't think that was it," Heather said. She stirred the bacon and the onions, in two different skillets, with the same spatula and decided to add a little more oil to the onions before throwing in the chopped spinach. She wouldn't make an omelet—scrambling would suffice—but spinach, onions, and cheese were matters of decency, as plain scrambled eggs would be too... jejune.

"Still obsessing over the murders in the Marks house and the disappearance of that boy you knew—"

"Bobby," Heather said. "Yes." Even with the fan on, the smoke from the bacon was thick. She opened the window above the sink. The skinny tree outside the window shook. She looked out, scanning. Probably a squirrel. "He—Bobby—was lost in this really weird kind of forest, and the trees were tearing him apart. When I woke up the first time, I didn't have any idea where he might have been. I simply..."

"Simply what?" Janet closed the laptop and angled her chair so she faced Heather more directly. She crossed her legs, most of which were visible beneath the high cut of her silky pajama bottoms. Janet sometimes took dance classes and jogged to stay in shape.

"I simply felt like I needed to be there, to protect him," Heather said. She poured the egg into the skillet with the onions and spinach. "Would you mind getting a couple of plates? They're in that cabinet."

As Janet obliged, she said, "You said the first time. Later, did you have an idea?"

"Huh?"

"You said the first time you woke up you didn't have any idea where—"

"Oh yeah," Heather said. She sprinkled cheese into the cooking egg concoction. "This morning, I remembered a conversation I had with Steven Marks."

Janet stood by Heather at the stove, holding the plates, which Heather didn't need yet. "Jesus, Heather, that doesn't seem like the kind of thing you'd forget."

"I never forgot, but... at the time, it didn't seem like anything important. It was a few years ago. Before the Marks boys were known for... anything. Steven was leaving Bobby's house as I was coming in to babysit. Bobby must have been in the bathroom or something. Steven kept saying what a good friend Bobby was. 'He's a really good guy, you know?' He must have said it three or four times."

Heather turned off the stove, took the plates from Janet, and served. Janet didn't need directions for getting the OJ out of the fridge and glasses from the cupboard. Soon they were sitting for a breakfast Heather felt sure was bigger than either of them usually ate.

"You said you didn't think Steven could have done anything to Bobby," Janet said. "That's a good reason."

Holding a piece of bacon near her mouth, Heather stared into space, remembering Steven Marks and remembering her dream.

Janet said, "But what does that have to do with the place where—"

"Does the term 'The Middle Reaches' mean anything to you?" Heather asked. She bit the bacon and chewed contemplatively.

"Sounds like something you do at the gym," Janet said, eating eggs. "You know, part of your abs routine. Stomach crunches. Middle reaches."

"I think it's a place," Heather said. "Steven said I should come see this 'really neat' place he and Bobby liked to go. Where Acton Way dead ends, and there's a woodsy area where the creek cuts through before another Acton Way begins."

"You think that's The Middle Reaches?"

"Yes. No. I don't know. It's related," Heather said. She finished her piece of bacon. "Maybe it's connected to... the place in my dream. And maybe...."

Janet swallowed eggs and gulped down OJ. "Maybe it's where Bobby disappeared?"

Heather nodded, but she didn't add, *Maybe it's where I have to go.*

Max

Standing by the window didn't feel right, but he wasn't ready to knock on the front door, not yet. What was he supposed to say? "Hi, I'm Max Gracey, and I can't really tell you anything about myself, but I know your name is Heather Park, and I want you to trust me enough to follow me to a place where a boy you knew might have been murdered." As introductions went, that wouldn't be the smoothest.

He didn't know the other girl. They were both probably older than he was, but the white girl looked younger than Heather. She had long, clean-shaven legs—pleasant—but her head was like a marble with a pixie haircut, which deflected his attention. Heather, on the other hand, standing at the stove, cracking eggs into a bowl, had elegance and perfect proportions.

Max didn't mind looking at her even though he felt like a Peeping Tom. Two girls in pajamas on a summer morning, with every reason to expect privacy, to expect that male eyes weren't evaluating, or savoring, or—

What *was* he doing? He couldn't hear what they were saying. The sounds of their voices, yes, but not the shapes of their words. The white girl's voice was higher pitched, whereas Heather's was more of an alto, more like—

Annie's.

Who was Annie?

The girl who broke your heart. She'd said, "The truth is that whatever I feel for you is irrelevant because you don't believe in me." And she'd told him to leave.

What hadn't he believed? Something about Bobby Lightfoot. Something about someone that made a goose walk across his grave. His hollow stomach ached. Something bad had happened to him. Something had happened to Annie, too—he didn't know, but he *knew*—and now he was here, in the bushes, by a tree too skinny to hide him if—

Heather looked out the window. He crouched, holding his breath. The window opened, and he pushed off the skinny tree to conceal himself more fully within the bushes by the side of the house. The tree shook, and Max winced.

Heather said, "He—Bobby—was lost in this really weird kind of forest, and the trees were tearing him apart. When I woke up the first time, I didn't have any idea where he might have been. I simply..."

Bobby? Was she already thinking about, and talking about, Bobby Lightfoot?

Max smelled bacon and onions. He didn't feel the slightest bit hungry. Staying in the bushes, too afraid of being seen to return to looking, he listened to the girls finish preparing breakfast. He listened to them talk about Bobby and someone named Steven Marks. "The Marks boys." He felt chills and more goosebumps. Then Heather mentioned "The Middle Reaches."

What did she know about The Middle Reaches? Did they, or it, call to her, too?

Heather mentioned the place between the two Acton Ways. Where he'd started. Where he... would take her. And he could tell by the way she talked about it that *she already wanted to go.*

Heather's white friend with the long legs said, "Maybe it's where Bobby disappeared?"

Maybe it's where I disappeared, Max thought. *Maybe it's where we all disappear.*

Bobby

The two dog-like creatures, their fur a yellow that seemed electrified in whatever light filled this place, came closer, slowly, deliberately. They didn't growl the same as before, but even their breathing sounded threatening, like they grinded the air in their throats as it passed down into their lungs. Their eyes, glowing red, were hardest to believe. This wasn't happening. This couldn't be happening.

Closer. Closer. *Closer.*

Bobby thought about jumping into the creek, but then he thought, *dogs can swim.* He kept thinking about running but knowing he couldn't run fast enough to get away. If these... things... wanted him, they would have him.

Closer. Closer. *Closer.*

Don't piss yourself. It's terribly important that you don't piss yourself.

Why? The smell of piss on the mangled corpse of a boy—

The dog-like creatures stood right in front of him now. Their jaws lolled, showing rows and rows of teeth. They breathed. Panted. Looked side to side. Looked at him. One at a time, Bobby made eye contact with them. They could have pounced. They didn't.

Bobby remembered a lesson from school. To make friends with a dog, to get yourself out of a tense situation, you let the dog smell your hand. Bobby extended his arm, trembling hand at the end of it, ready to see the hand bitten off. He held the shaking hand up to the stretched muzzle of one of the dog-creatures.

It sniffed and looked at him.

He held his hand to the other creature's nose. It sniffed and bowed its head.

Bobby extended the same shaking hand further. Was he crazy? He set the hand on the bowed head. He stroked it. He scratched behind the pointed ears. The fur was matted and rough, but also... fluffy. Bobby stepped closer to the two dog-creatures and put a hand on each one's head, petting them. One of them sighed, contented.

He couldn't believe what was happening, but Bobby was, indeed, making friends.

EPISODE 19: KIND STRANGERS OF THE STRANGEST KIND

Janet

The doorbell rang. Heather was still in the shower, and Janet sat in the kitchen, drinking coffee, still wearing her PJs, which she'd worn for spending time with Heather, not for entertaining... uninvited guests.

"HEATHER!" she yelled. "SOMEBODY'S AT THE DOOR!"

Heather showered with the bathroom door open so things wouldn't get unbearably steamy—this house had shitty circulation—which meant they could hear each other. "I'LL BE OUT IN A MINUTE! WOULD YOU SEE WHO IT IS?"

"Christ," Janet muttered, setting her mug on the breakfast table. She was on her way when the doorbell rang a second time. "Hold on, hold on, I'm getting there!"

She opened the front door. Her self-consciousness about wearing silky, skimpy jam-jams doubled. The boy standing on Heather's narrow front porch was objectively good-looking, maybe a little younger than she was—sixteen, maybe—wearing all black, maybe goth but with a contradictory summer tan—and he had a faun-like look in his eyes that Janet didn't trust.

"Hi," he said. He seemed pleasant, but an aspect of his

pleasantry, which she could not pinpoint, seemed fake. "Is Heather at home?"

When you show up to visit someone, you ring the bell and then ask if they're home. The behavior was normal... for like 1950!!! Who shows up unexpectedly at someone's door these days? When not too many blocks over, kids are getting killed, and—

"Heather is... *indisposed*," Janet said. She sounded so stupid.

"Hi," the boy said again. This time he held out his hand. "My name's Max Gracey."

He expected a handshake! She looked at his extended hand as she said, "I'm Janet." She considered for a moment before she added, "Fillion."

The boy retracted his hand and rubbed his smooth cheeks as he said, "It's nice to meet you, Janet Fillion. Do you think Heather will be up for a visit?"

"I don't know," Janet said. "You'll have to ask her." Janet withdrew her head from the doorway, listening for the shower— still on. "Later."

She closed the door in the boy's face, locked it, and walked back toward the kitchen.

"WHO WAS IT?" Heather yelled.

"SOME BOY WHO WANTED TO SEE YOU!"

"DID YOU INVITE HIM IN?" Heather sounded annoyed, as if she knew Janet had shut the door in the boy's face and as if having done so were unequivocally wrong.

"UH... NO?"

"GIVE HIM SOME GODDAMNED COFFEE AND TELL HIM TO WAIT FIVE FUCKING MINUTES!"

Less than a minute later, Janet Fillion and Max Gracey sat

at the breakfast table, each with a mug of coffee. Janet hadn't apologized. Heather would never know.

"So, how do you know Heather?" Janet asked. Nothing wrong with doing a little background work.

"Oh, she... she... I mean, her reputation proceeds her, doesn't it?" Max said. It was an odd thing to say.

"What... do... you... *mean?*" Janet asked, putting her elbows on the table and leaning in.

"I mean...." An awkward pause if ever there was an awkward pause. The summer tan on the boy's face got a little whiter. That tilted smile that probably worked on lots of girls got twitchy. "I mean at school. Everybody's heard of her."

That was true. Second in her graduating class—Salutatorian—and then off to the Ivy League, people knew about her. But knowing about was different from knowing. Did Max Gracey's answer mean he didn't actually *know* Heather? "Heard of her? You mean you—"

"To be honest, she probably doesn't remember me," Max said.

Janet considered rising so fast she'd knock her chair over while she threw hot coffee in his face. He'd gotten inside on false pretenses! Except he'd never said anything false...

"Who are you, exactly?" Janet asked, eying the knife rack near the sink. She was fast. She could get to it.

Max

Everything was going wrong! He'd spent so long working up his nerve to ring the doorbell, and he'd convinced himself that they'd be nice, and it'd all be fine, and from the first second when she'd opened the door, she'd seemed to know he didn't belong, that he deserved to be shut out, that Heather would be better off if she never laid eyes on him—

41

He did his best to answer her questions, but she was interrogating him. He didn't have the resources to dodge her for long, but he had to try, except then she asked the one question that baffled him most: "Who are you, exactly?"

Max stared into his coffee, using all his strength to keep his composure. "Nobody," he said.

Janet stood, carrying her coffee, and crossed the kitchen to the sink. "Can you be more specific?"

Max kept his eyes on Janet as he said, "I'm just a guy here with a message for Heather Park."

He didn't know what the right thing to say might have been, but that wasn't it. Janet put down her coffee and grabbed a chef's knife from the rack. Pointing the knife at him, she cut the distance between them in half. "No, you're just a guy getting the hell out of here. You're done with the coffee, now leave."

Max considered telling her that he hadn't drunk any of his coffee, but he decided she wouldn't be fazed. He held up his hands, maintained his most charming smile, and said, "Hey, I'm harmless. I only want to talk to Heather."

"What part of 'get the hell out of here' don't you understand?" Janet jabbed the air in front of her with the knife.

Flummoxed, Max let his jaw drop, speechless. Janet also seemed to struggle with finding the words that would advance them from their increasingly awkward predicament—or maybe to struggle with the possibility of a knife-attack, he couldn't be sure.

Heather walked in wearing long white shorts and a hot pink shirt, rubbing her wet hair with a big green towel. She stopped when she saw Janet with the knife. She turned and made eye contact with Max and said, "This is our guest?"

"I asked him to leave," Janet said.

"Why aren't you leaving?" Heather asked.

"I have to talk to you," Max answered. "My name's Max." He tried to hold eye contact with her as much as possible, to establish intimacy, to make a connection.

"Did Max do anything *untoward?*" Heather asked. She kept looking at him.

"He's creepy," Janet answered.

"Don't let down your guard, then," Heather said. She crossed to the breakfast table and put her towel on the back of a chair. Taking a step back, maintaining eye contact, she said, "What do you want to talk about? And be brief. Your other options are the knife or the cops. Or both, I suppose."

Max had exactly one move to make, and he decided to make it now. "Call the cops, or anyone else, and I'll go, and you'll never know what I have to tell you about Bobby Lightfoot."

The girls' heads made slow turns so they could look at each other before looking back at him.

Janet said, "Did he just say—"

"He did," Heather said.

"How did he know we—"

"I don't know," Heather said, reestablishing eye contact with him. "But you're right. He's creepy." Her eyes said something more, though. He had her hooked.

Heather

As soon as Max said "Bobby Lightfoot," a word popped into Heather's head, and it stayed there. Kismet. Max showing up, the same interest uniting the three of them—kismet. She knew where they were going, but she waited for destiny to play out.

Janet snagged the closest chair from the breakfast table and dragged it across the kitchen tiles. She sat too far for Max to grab her but close enough to reach him with a knife-lunge. Her facial expression was fierce. Heather had to suppress a smile. "So," Janet said, "tell us what you know."

Heather wasn't ready to sit yet. "You want us to believe you know more than the cops, more than anyone in the neighborhood, even his family—"

"I... don't know," Max said. Looking at the *aw shucks* vacancy in his cow-ish eyes, Heather believed him.

"The only person who could know more would be the one who took him," Janet said, brandishing the knife. "The one who killed him. Did you kill him?"

"No!" The answer was immediate, laced with offense. "I mean, I don't know, but I think I'd know." He took several deep breaths, calming. "Look, all I know—"

"You don't know much," Janet interjected. Heather wanted to flash her a look to let her know she wasn't helping, but she kept her eyes on Max's eyes as his attempts at calming breaths became faster and faster heaving.

"It's okay, Max," Heather said in her most soothing voice. Janet turned to her with a face that said WTF. "Tell me what you have to tell me."

"Actually..." and his breathing calmed, "it's what I have to show you."

Kismet! "It's more than that," Heather said.

"It's where I have to take you," Max said.

Heather took the seat at the table across from Max. "Sweetwater Creek," she said. "The place between the two Acton Ways."

Janet gawked at her.

"Yes," Max said.

"The Middle Reaches," Heather said.

"Yes," Max said.

Heather felt like a charlatan psychic befuddled by her pretended clairvoyancy's complete accuracy. After years of pretending, she'd somehow become the real thing.

Janet looked like Heather had just eaten her pet gerbil.

"Max, I need to talk to Janet alone," Heather said. "Will you wait on the front porch?"

Max stood, keeping his eyes on hers. Pretty eyes. Good complexion. He looked at Janet, who sat with the knife like a gatekeeper on the path through the kitchen toward the front door. Heather looked at Janet, caught her gaze, then looked at the knife, which Janet lowered. Max walked by and exited. Heather listened to the front door open and close.

Janet hurried out of the kitchen. Heather heard the front door's bolt and chain slide into their places. Janet hurried back in and sat in her chair before pulling it closer to the table. "What... the... *hell*, Heather? You can't seriously be thinking about going somewhere with this freakazoid who just shows up on your doorstep?"

"The coincidence is amazing, isn't it? We're talking about the place at the dead end and a place called The Middle Reaches, and he shows up wanting to go there with us—"

"Bullshit, Heather!" Janet's passion climbed. "You fed him all of that! I bet before you mentioned it, he wasn't thinking about Acton Way, or The Middle Reaches, or, or, or anything but getting you somewhere..."

"Somewhere?"

"Somewhere where nobody'll hear you scream and it's easy to hide the body!" Janet seemed shocked by her own words, which hardly stirred Heather at all.

"You don't have to come with me if you don't want to," Heather said.

"What?"

"I said—"

"I pretty much got the feeling I wasn't invited," Janet said, sulky.

"Consider yourself invited," Heather said. "I won't go if you don't go. Our new friend Max will have to live with that. Remember our toast? To making new discoveries *together*."

"Together," Janet said. She looked down and saw the knife in her hand. She lurched as if it surprised her and set it on the breakfast table. "I need time to shower and get dressed."

"I feel confident that he'll wait," Heather said. She smiled at her friend. She thought of putting her hand on Janet's exposed knee but decided not to.

Janet still looked mopey. "I don't feel good about this. What if he has other boys waiting to ambush us or something?"

"He doesn't," Heather said. "I think he's perfectly sincere. Weird, but sincere. Come on, it'll be the investigation we talked about. An adventure."

Mopey morphed into pouty. "*Moby Dick* was an adventure. Look how that turned out."

"You've been reading *way* too much of the AP English summer list." Heather went to get her hairbrush from the bathroom before Janet went in to shower. The matter was settled.

Bobby

At first, he thought it was a mirage. Then he thought it was a threat.

Bobby followed the creek, an uber-dog at each side. His companions took getting used to, and he hadn't made the full adjustment yet. The problem was that they looked, well, evil.

Glowing red eyes, a preponderance of teeth, bonus legs... they belonged in the *Monster Manual* for sure. But they were being nice to him, and that was a comfort in this screwy place.

Seeing the form ahead, downstream, wearing the familiar blue and white striped polo, was not comforting. A mist hung over the ground and to his right, over the water, so the first counterargument had been that the image of the form was like another image on the water, reflection-illusion, not there in any way but projected to disturb his mind.

The second counterargument—and he was counterarguing before he understood that the argument was that The Man in the Grinning Mask, a master of mirrors, was coming to him in this disguise that he couldn't understand—was that a real boy was walking up the creek to meet him.

Bobby and his companions stopped. The form in the familiar shirt continued to approach. "Hello!" Bobby called.

"Hey!" the form replied. He sounded like a boy, like a teenager whose voice had already dropped, anyway. "Am I to understand that you are Bobby Lightfoot himself, here, in person?"

The form kept getting closer. The uber-dogs didn't react, which was a good sign. Since they hadn't torn him to pieces, Bobby expected the uber-dogs to protect him. He didn't know why that made sense, but it did. "Yeah. Who are you?"

The form—he—was almost close enough that he didn't have to shout. "My name's Sheldon! They told me to come out here and meet you!"

"Who's 'they?'" Bobby shot back.

Sheldon got into normal talking range and stopped. "Hell if I know. All I know is, around here, if you get told to do something, sooner or later, you'll end up doing it, so why fight it, right? Besides, it's nice to meet someone of the human and I'm hoping relatively sane variety." Sheldon extended his hand for shaking.

Booby took a reluctant step, another, and several more, easier steps, as his companions advanced with him. He grasped Sheldon's hand and shook it. "Nice to meet you, Sheldon. I'm Bobby, but you seem to know that already."

"Yeah, well, after a while, the whispers and screams and all the stuff you hear, some of it makes sense." Sheldon gave their surroundings a haunted look that Bobby didn't like. "Anyway," Sheldon continued, brightening, "I'm here to make sure you get where you need to be. The Middle Reaches can be a scary place. You know, being scared isn't as scary when you're not alone."

"I agree," Bobby said. He examined Sheldon, felt warmth. Sheldon had... charm.

"And who," Sheldon said, kneeling, "are these guys?" He put a hand on each of the uber-dogs' heads and petted them playfully. When one of them snapped at his fingers, he didn't seem to mind.

"They're... I think of them as uber-dogs. I guess they're my friends," Bobby said.

"Do your friends have names?"

"Uh... no," Bobby said.

"Well," Sheldon said, addressing the uber-dog on Bobby's left. "You have a scar on your... I guess that's a nose... and you," he addressed the uber-dog on Bobby's right, "don't." He turned to left and right respectively: "You shall be Thing One, and you shall be Thing Two."

Bobby didn't know which he liked more, the reference to *The Cat in the Hat* or the possibility that Sheldon also looked at the uber-dogs and thought of John Carpenter's *The Thing*. Either way, Bobby had the impression that he and Sheldon would get along.

Sheldon

He and Bobby followed the creek, Thing One and Thing Two at their sides. They learned about each other. Sheldon had lived on Acton Way, with Sweetwater Creek running through his backyard. Bobby's friend Steven lived on Acton Way, where they played a lot in an overgrown area behind the creek in his backyard. Bobby and his friends hung out between the two Acton Ways. So did Sheldon and his friends.

Sheldon quickly recognized that Bobby was a boy who'd gone missing years before Sheldon himself had... relocated... and that the "Steven" he mentioned was Steven Marks, and the house on Acton Way where Bobby used to play was infamous for the murders Steven and his brother Gordon had committed there.

These details were not to be mentioned. Whatever the order of events, there or here, *here*, Bobby was a newcomer. He deserved an adjustment period without being overcrowded by facts.

Sheldon and the shorter, rounder, younger boy walked side by side along the creek like new best friends, diving into each other's lives. They both read a great deal, both far beyond their grade levels, and both enjoyed classic horror and science fiction. They both told stories connected to the area between the Acton Ways, and they both told stories about other places, beyond.

Sheldon talked about the Cavern of The Mouth, the Gate, and some of the wonders where they were going. Bobby remained phlegmatic. Sheldon understood. The boy was too much like himself. He knew the unknown held terrors. He knew wonders weren't cheap. Why were they, two forms from the same mold, a pair? What did The Middle Reaches—or whatever master gave the orders—want from them?

Heather

The steps up to Heather's dad's front door were barely wide enough for Heather to sit on the top one beside Max without being awkwardly close. She sat, though, and said, "I'll come with you, but Janet's coming too, and she needs some time to get ready."

"Fine," Max said. He squinted as he looked toward her, the sun in his eyes. The skin above his nose wrinkled in an adorable way.

Adorable? What was he, like... sixteen? Sixteen and nineteen wouldn't exactly be May-December, but sixteen seemed like a long time ago from Heather's perspective. Was she perverse for finding this... boy... attractive? His shoulders were broad enough. He filled out his T-shirt and jeans in a way that wasn't exactly childish. But still. She had to question herself.

"You live nearby?" she asked.

He shrugged.

"How long have you been interested in Bobby's... disappearance?"

"This morning," he said.

"What sparked the interest? Did you stumble upon some information, or...?"

"It... occurred to me. What about you? Why the interest?" Clouds passed over the sun. He looked at her without squinting.

"I'd pass it off as morbid curiosity, a little driven by the fact that I knew him. But... I have this feeling, you know? Like I'm supposed to look?" She studied his face. Not even a flinch of doubt.

"I know," he said.

Kismet! She and Janet were meant to go with this

adorable boy on this *adventure*.

EPISODE 20: TALES OF THE KING

Sheldon

Bobby's description of The Man in the Grinning Mask made Sheldon recall a man from dreams—possibly visions—but that man and The Man who stalked Bobby couldn't be the same, because Sheldon knew the man he had seen, not his name but who he was... underneath. The Cavern had told him.

The main connection was red: The Man in the Grinning Mask wore a red cape, and the man Sheldon had seen wore a bright red shirt. They were both tall and agile. Bobby's Man was thin. Sheldon's man was thin when he was younger, broad and muscular later, at a time Sheldon dared to think of as *the present*.

Both men enjoyed killing.

They both had connections to The Middle Reaches, but Sheldon could only speculate about what brought The Man in the Grinning Mask here. The man in the red shirt, however, had come *from* here. He had issued from The Mouth. His home was Carcosa.

Bobby thought he'd read something about Carcosa, but he didn't really remember. Sheldon told him about the Lost City and the Walled City, about Lake Hali and the poisoned, burning mists. He told him about the three gods, each King of a domain, God of the Lake, God the Citadel, and God of the Palace.

The gods visited their reality through avatars. Sheldon

knew nothing of the God of the Lake. He knew little of the God of the Palace, who was High King, the King in Yellow, Hastur—except that it chose politicians and lawyers as avatars, representatives uninterested in casual victims. The God of the Citadel, however, had a less particular sadistic streak. It enjoyed random sacrifice. Mass murder. Serial killing.

An avatar of the God of the Citadel, the man in the red shirt lurked in family places. The first time Sheldon saw him, he was young and thin and didn't look terribly out of place, wandering alone in the evening at a county fair, a temporary setup with exhibits, games, and rides.

Walking through an alley of games, he looked at a boy using a squirt gun to shoot a steady stream of water into a painted clown's mouth. He giggled as he aimed. The girl beside him, a teenager, looked bored. The way Red Shirt's eyes moved over them—other people might not feel it—but Sheldon felt a nauseating sense of... predatory appraisal. Would these children die tonight?

He exited the area with the games without appearing to make a selection and moved toward the rides. A carousel played loud ragtime that severed its surroundings from the moment—this could be any carousel at any fair anywhere in America at any moment in the last century.

The carousel received reinforcement from the Ferris wheel towering beside it, on which mostly young couples rode, making out near the top as if no one could see them. Red Shirt saw them. He watched the wheel spin, tracking three couples, then two, then one.

They were a white couple about Sheldon's age, or the age Sheldon appeared to be. The boy had short, dark brown hair, and the girl had long blonde hair and glasses. They both wore clothes a little too fancy for a county fair, collars and buttons and belts, he in pleated slacks, she in a long skirt—dressed to impress one another on a formal date? Sheldon had never done such a thing.

When the couple disembarked the wheel, Red Shirt began to follow them. He was quite good at blending in and out of passing groups, stopping to study an attraction with indistinct interest, and otherwise remaining invisible. Sheldon didn't know yet that the couple's pursuer was a god, but he strongly suspected that the man in the red shirt wasn't a man.

Soon, the couple's trajectory suggested that their evening was ending. Arm in arm, they walked toward the parking lot. Red Shirt continued to follow, closing the distance. By the time the couple was walking under the arched sign that marked both entrance and exit, he couldn't avoid being out in the open, clearly moving, as the couple was, toward the parking lot.

In the parking lot they were alone, two in the lead, one not very far behind. Why didn't the girl glance back over her shoulder? She must have felt Red Shirt's eyes on her. The boy, too. The eyes weren't predatory. That phase was over. They were intent. Focused. Task-oriented. Red Shirt had reduced the couple to a *task*.

The boy shoved a hand in one of his pants pockets. Red Shirt did the same. The boy took out a key ring that included a rectangle with buttons for controlling car locks and—maybe a panic button? Other people weren't too far off. A blaring car alarm might save them. Not that Sheldon really expected this situation to work out in their favor—

Red Shirt took something out of his pocket that looked like a polished wooden handle with nothing attached.

The boy pressed a button, and lights on a nearby car flashed. The couple split, the girl going to the passenger's side, the boy to the driver's.

Red Shirt crouched and ran. He bumped into the boy, who looked at him, annoyed, as Red Shirt opened one of the rear doors and got into the back seat. The couple didn't have time to process what had happened; their brains finished executing their most recent commands; they got into the car.

Sheldon noticed the polished wooden handle's metal edge a second before Red Shirt unfolded it. It was a straight razor. He held it to the boy's throat. In an affectless voice, he told the couple to close their doors.

They obeyed.

After the doors slammed, Red Shirt wasted no time. He slit the boy's throat and held on to him as he gargled in surprise and grasped at the resulting gush. The girl screamed, and a second later she had her door open and was trying to dive out.

Red Shirt released the boy, grabbed her arm, and yanked her far enough back into the vehicle to make her bump into her erstwhile companion, who slumped toward his closed door. He seemed too busy bleeding to offer help. The girl tried freeing the arm Red Shirt held while bashing him with her available fist. The result was little more than squirming. Her glasses fell crookedly across her face.

Red Shirt said something about how upset she must be after losing what's-his-name. His voice remained affectless, but he smiled as he sliced open her wrist, two horizontal cuts.

She looked from her bleeding wrist to the still-open car door. "I don't wanna die," she said.

With one hand, he sliced a third line across her wrist. With the other, he placed a finger over his lips. "Shhhhh."

"I don't wanna die!" she said, louder. Then, again and again, louder and louder: "I don't wanna die, I don't wanna die, I don't wanna die, I don't wanna—"

He slashed her throat.

When Sheldon finished telling Bobby about his first dream, or vision, of the God of the Citadel's avatar, Bobby was quiet for a moment before he asked, "Why did you tell me that? What good could knowing that possibly do me?"

"You need to know what's out here," Sheldon said, not

knowing why he'd told the story but knowing that telling it was right. "Not all monsters are like Thing One and Thing Two."

"Yeah," Bobby said. "I knew that already."

Gordon

Gordon didn't know why, but searching through The Middle Reaches, layer after layer, he didn't think about Ellie, even though he had a hard-on most of the time, and Ellie knew how to take care of that. He thought about Adam. Finding Adam. What Adam would think of him now. Whether Adam would accept Steven. What Adam understood about this place. How he was connected to it.

Gordon felt sure that Adam was connected to The Middle Reaches.

Adam had two kinds of knowledge, or two kinds that he seemed interested in passing on to Gordon. The first was the kind of knowledge he shared around Ellie, when husband and wife were being mock parents, the NIMBY kind of knowledge that Keeps Killing Safe. The second was a deeper... wisdom. Adam got a starry look when he talked about it.

For a while Gordon was going to Adam and Ellie's house for lunch almost every day, and sometimes Adam would give these little lessons. Following the creek with Steven, Gordon thought about sitting with Adam and Ellie at their kitchen table, eating sandwiches while Adam, tall, bulky Adam in one of his signature bright-red shirts, talked about the importance of separating sex from murder.

"First of all, all sex is inherently unsanitary," Adam said. "The bush and the vagina, they capture things. Your hairs, about which we'll have more to say later, or just a follicle, or skin cells, or the slightest bit of fluid... dangerous terrain, perilous. No offense to your vagina, dear."

"None taken," Ellie said. "Sometimes, they have teeth."

"I would rather," Adam said, in his usual, unfeeling, matter-of-fact way, "fuck a woman to death with a knife while masturbating in my pants than actually insert my penis in a woman I plan to kill. I hope you don't feel like I'm being too misogynistic, hon. I am illustrating a point."

"Misogynistic or not, your point is one I agree with. I'd much rather you insert a knife than your penis, which I happen to consider my property," Ellie said.

"A broader point to consider, and you definitely should never overlook this," Adam said, taking a bite of his sandwich, "is that men in the heat of passion usually do not think clearly. Not thinking clearly while committing murder leads to incarceration and/or execution. Q. E. D."

Ellie stood. "Well, since we're Q.E.D.-ing, I'm going to go change shirts so the mayo I dropped on this one doesn't leave permanent grease stains. Gentlemen, I trust you can entertain each other."

"I imagine we can," Adam said.

Gordon nodded, secretly hoping Adam would do just what he would do. Ellie left the room.

"You listening, champ?" Adam said.

Gordon nodded again.

Adam leaned forward confidentially. "If you're ever in that situation," he said, and he looked left and right before looking into Gordon's eyes. Adam's blankness seemed almost... giddy. "Fucking a woman to death with a knife, I mean."

Gordon smiled. "And jerking off at the same time?"

"Of course," Adam said. He had that starry look. Black stars. Gordon understood now that Adam sparkled with black stars. "When you're about to come, and she's about to die— which should happen at about the same time—make sure you look at her face. Not just her eyes. The way her nostrils flap. The corners of her mouth. A little smile, maybe? A little smile, right as death comes?"

Right as death comes. How many times had Gordon jerked off, thinking of himself as death when he came?

Janet

They walked up and down the hills of Fairview, the main street leading out of Rolling Vistas, toward Acton Way. Janet had suggested that she or Heather drive—make "Max" sit in the back seat—but Heather had said it was a nice morning for a walk. Under the bright blue sky, the creepy newcomer did seem less threatening. Just as creepy, but not anything she and Heather couldn't handle.

Even though they all knew where they were going, Max led, staying out in front, while Janet and Heather stayed as a pair a short distance behind. The spacing was enough to make Janet feel like they could have a conversation without the boy butting in. "I didn't mention it last night," Janet said, "you know, because we were blocking out reality-scary stuff, but I did some research."

Heather looked ahead as if Max might be about to do something interesting. "Oh? What kind of research?"

"I wanted to know more about what you told me," Janet said. "About Steven and Gordon Marks. About Bobby Lightfoot. Did you know the public library keeps copies of yearbooks from all the nearby schools?"

"Never occurred to me," Heather said.

"I thought they might be difficult to get to, with all the media interest and local curiosity. You know there are already websites springing up about the Marks boys and that basement." Some of the websites were disturbing, treating Gordon and

Steven Marks like cult heroes. Slightly more disturbing, some suggested that strange abominations continued to occur in the Markses' house.

"I've seen some things online, yeah," Heather said.

Heather sounded too far away. "Okay, well, my point is that, despite all that garbage, I was able to get to the yearbooks and see pictures. Bobby always looks... looked... so serious. Steven looked like a goofball. Gordon.... I don't know, I could be projecting. I didn't recognize him from school. I thought he looked... dead-eyed."

"Makes sense," Heather said.

"What?"

"I said it makes sense for a boy like that to have something... missing," Heather said.

Heather still seemed too distant. "Seeing the pictures made it all more, I don't know, concrete, but I guess I didn't learn much that was new about them. Looking through newspapers, though, I did learn something else." Janet looked to Heather for her response.

"What's that?" Heather faced forward.

Janet looked away. "Maybe nothing," she said. "I don't want to bore you."

Heather looked at her. "You won't *bore* me. Please. I want to know."

Janet tried not to smile. "You ever hear of the Mortimers?"

Heather kept looking at her. "The—what? Who? No."

Ahead of them, Max reached the point where Fairview Street met Acton Way. He turned right and, remaining visible, walked the short distance to the Dead End sign. He waited.

"The Mortimers," Janet said. "Adam and Eleanor. Thirty-something couple, lived in a house on the other side of where we're going. At the beginning of the other Acton Way. The police were looking for them in connection with the murders. What the Marks boys did. Cops said nothing to the press about why."

"That's kind of unusual, isn't it?"

"Questioning, all they would say is questioning," Janet said. "People speculated that the cops found something incriminating in the couple's house, but nobody could confirm. What's really unusual is that nobody could find pictures of Adam or Eleanor. There was a police sketch of Adam, taken from one of the neighbors. Made him look like every other thirty-something white guy."

They stopped at the end of Fairview. Max stood at the Dead End sign, looking at them but not moving to intrude. He could probably hear them anyway.

"What do you think?" Heather asked. "Do you think they were involved?"

"I had this crazy idea," Janet said. "We talked about how hard to believe what Gordon and Steven did was, because they were so young. And Adam and Eleanor disappeared around the same time as Gordon and Steven. So what if... what if they were, like, guides? Encouraging them, fanning the flames? What if they were like—" and she'd given this phrase some thought —"mentors in murder?"

"That's a scary thought," Heather said. "Not crazy, but scary. It makes this whole thing seem... bigger." She looked at Max, who studied the ground. "Are you ready to keep going?"

Since Heather asked, yes, she was ready. Heather looked impressed, and Janet felt satisfied.

Heather

The area between the two Acton Ways, where the creek from the Markses' back yard swelled to swimmable size, sucked a lot of the atmosphere out of the "adventure" she and Janet had started with adorable Max. It was too pretty to seem dangerous. It looked like an ideal picnic spot. Tall trees bursting with green surrounded it. Heather peered through, toward the other side.

"Do you know which one?" Heather asked.

"Which one what?" Max asked, looking at the creek, downstream, where the light seemed weaker.

"Which house was, or is, the Mortimers'?" Heather said, looking to Janet.

"No," Janet said, stretching for views of the other Acton Way from different angles. "I bet it's that one, though." She pointed at the house closest to the other dead end. They had a narrow view of its back deck, which had sliding glass doors.

Heather nudged Max so he would look where Janet pointed. "Do you know anything about that house? Ever heard of Adam and Eleanor Mortimer?"

Max looked, and some of the color left his face. "See you later, Max," he muttered.

"What?" Janet demanded. "Speak so others can hear you."

"Nothing," Max said. "Goosebumps. That old saying, 'a goose just walked over my grave.' It's creepy. Like me, I guess."

"Yeah, like you," Janet said.

"So, you don't know about the house," Heather said. "Or the Mortimers."

"No," Max said, and he walked to the creek and moved alongside it, in the direction of the current. "I know we go this way."

"This place wasn't your big reveal," Janet said. "Not the reason you wanted us to follow you."

"No," Max said, moving slowly enough for them to catch up at any moment.

Heather had an odd question in her head, odder still because she knew what the answer would be. "You've never been where you're taking us, have you?"

"No," Max said. "At least, I don't think so. But I know we follow the creek."

"To The Middle Reaches," Heather said.

"Yes," Max said.

Heather moved toward him. "You still buying this shit?" Janet said, staying still.

"Adventure," Heather said, motioning Janet along. Heather caught up to Max's side.

"We should have used bug spray," Janet said, catching up to Heather's other side. Janet wore short shorts again—her legs would be a feast for mosquitos, especially so close to the water. Heather felt for her, but not enough to turn back. Besides, even though she wore longer shorts, she wouldn't be much better off. And Max wore all black. They were ill-prepared for a summer walk through Southern woods.

The blue sky above them faded, grey-ish white seeping in. The trees' leaves seemed less vibrant. "You know about Bobby Lightfoot," Heather said, engaging Janet's attention before eying Max. They were both asking him questions. They were a team. Janet needed to feel that. "Do you know about Gordon and Steven Marks?"

Max rubbed his exposed forearm, the one closest to her. Heather thought she could see the hairs standing on end. "Goosebumps?" she asked.

"I guess maybe their names are familiar," Max said. "Markses, Mortimers. Whoever they are, I don't think we want to run into them while we're here."

Heather exchanged knowing glances with Janet. The atmosphere of adventure was returning. She caught a whiff of honeysuckle, felt a stir in her chest and between her thighs, looked at Max, and surprised herself by thinking, *Maybe not adventure. With any luck, a good, old-fashioned, hardcore f—*

Steven

With help from Gordon, who heard things' names when Steven only heard whispers, chatter, and screams, Steven had started to build a map in his mind. The place where he used to play with Bobby and Chris, the place between the Acton Ways, they called the Outer Reaches.

When the sky faded from blue into greyish-white, they were in the Border Region. When it was pink with shocks of red, they were in The Middle Reaches, the First Layers. If the sky was darker red, picking up purple, they were in the Middle Layers. The sky Steven knew best—with the black stars—was in the Inner Layers.

The Inner Layers led to the Cavern of the Mouth, which they would enter, soon—but not yet.

Steven and Gordon were in the Inner Layers when they switched off, blackout, and reappeared in the Border Region, familiar grey-ish white above them. They stood between high tufts of bramble and the trees, the creek beyond the bramble, and with the creek—

"Get down," Gordon whispered, pulling Steven to his knees. Steven knelt by the bushes, and his brother crouched with him. Steven understood. They weren't alone. Three people walked along the other side of the creek, not far upstream from them.

Gordon turned away as if something beside him, something Steven couldn't see, had wiped out other interests. Steven remained intrigued by the first other people they'd encountered in—he didn't know how long—and peeked through the bramble.

"You know about Bobby Lightfoot," one girl, or young woman, said. She was pretty and Asian. Her voice sounded in charge. She looked familiar. She knew about Bobby? She continued, "Do you know about Gordon and Steven Marks?" She knew about *them*? Why was she asking about *them*?

Memory clicked. She was Bobby's old babysitter! Steven couldn't remember her name....

The babysitter looked at the boy beside her. He looked familiar, too. "Goosebumps?" she asked.

Max! The boy's name was Max! He'd been Annie Ledbetter's boyfriend. "I guess maybe their names are familiar," Max said. "Markses, Mortimers. Whoever they are, I don't think we want to run into them while we're here."

Gordon laughed. "No, you don't, Max. You most definitely don't." He turned toward Steven, holding an item in each hand. Both items were a little muddy—Gordon had undoubtedly found them on the ground—but they were easy enough to see.

One of them was a hatchet. Gordon gave it to Steven, who liked its weight in his hand. The other item was a polished wooden handle. It didn't seem like anything else, except Steven saw the metal edge that could probably fold out. A pocketknife?

Gordon unfolded the blade. "It's a straight razor," Gordon said, grinning. "I think... I think Adam left these here for us. He wants us... we've got... a purpose. Here. With them."

Steven understood.

"Are you ready?" Gordon asked. "Are you with me?"

Steven looked at the hatchet. Yes, he was ready, and yes, he was with his brother. The moment had come for the hunters to meet their prey.

EPISODE 21: SHADOW PEOPLE

Heather

"Over there," Janet said, using her eyes to direct Heather's attention slightly ahead of them, across the creek.

"I don't see anything," Heather said. She wouldn't say what she felt. "The change in the weather must be getting to you." She felt like they were being watched, and the feeling wasn't the weather, even though the sky's quick transition from blue to dull white was unnerving. The trees were different, too, like they were preparing for autumn. All the bushes had thorns. Thin vines wove through them.

The temperature was dropping. Not much, but a little. The smell of honeysuckle—with something unsettling beneath it—remained strong.

"That bush over there is shaking," Max said. "Like something jostled it."

"We're in the freaking woods," Heather said. "It could have been a squirrel or, I don't know, at worst a coyote. But I don't think they make it this far into the suburbs."

"I trust Janet more than I trust this place," Max said. "It isn't the weather."

Interesting! "I trust Janet." Heather had detected nothing but animosity between her two traveling companions, so Max's declaration suggested development. They all might get along. That could be... promising. "Okay, Janet," Heather said, "what do you think you saw?"

And what did Max mean by "It isn't the weather?" *What* wasn't the weather? Whatever Janet saw? Or the change in the sky, which didn't seem to involve clouds, simply a... shift... in color?

She thought of Bobby Lightfoot, Steven Marks, and Chris Ledbetter, who pretended to have adventures in different dimensions connected to the area between the Acton Ways. Different dimensions. As if they were walking through a different dimension! Dimension X, Bobby called it, like something from a comic book. Could The Middle Reaches be Dimension X?

Janet seemed reluctant to respond. "I... it was probably my imagination getting the better of me."

"Now you have to tell us," Heather said. She stopped walking when the bushes that captivated Janet and Max were almost directly across the creek. The others stopped, and they all looked together.

"If he was there, he's gone, or at least better hidden," Janet said.

Heather tried to stay patient. "*Who?*"

"I... thought I recognized Gordon Marks's face," Janet said. Neither one of them had ever met the boy, but Janet had looked at yearbook pictures... apparently, enough yearbook pictures, for long enough, to think she would know the face at a distance, peering through leaves and branches and thorny vines—

"We should keep moving," Max said. He had his hand on his stomach.

"Good idea," Janet said. They moved downstream, leaving a space between them wide enough for Heather while Heather lingered, staring at the bushes across the creek. Did she *want* to catch a glimpse of Gordon Marks? Seeing him there... him being there at all... wouldn't be good for them. She'd told Janet she wanted to see a recording of what had happened in the Markses' basement. Seeing Gordon would be... a move in that direction.

One of the bushes shook as if something, or someone, jostled it. In her head, an unfamiliar voice said, "How's Annie?"

Max: "Goosebumps. That old saying, 'a goose just walked over my grave.' It's creepy."

Heather hurried to catch up with the others.

Janet

She felt better about Max but worse about her decision to come here. Investigative journalism—real reporters went into war zones, compared to which, this place was—what? An eerie patch of woods in the suburbs. The *privileged* suburbs. She shouldn't have a problem being here. But her gut said—and she trusted her gut—this place was deeper shit than she could handle.

Other parts of her knew Heather was here, and Heather meant *ache*. She'd wanted Heather for a long time, but the want had never been so total. She felt it everywhere. In her arms. In her fingertips. She couldn't abandon Heather, and furthermore, along with Heather, she felt—

and it must have been related to her journalist side, even though it seemed different—

an overwhelming desire to *know*. Where the hell would they end up? Would they really learn something about Bobby Lightfoot?

Had she really heard someone splash into the creek behind them?

Don't look. Don't give in to your imagination.

She thought of that movie *The Vanishing*, the foreign version, which she'd seen at Heather's dad's house before Heather left for college. A guy's girlfriend disappears, and he spends years looking for her. Finally, this other guy shows up and tells the first guy he can find out what happened—only if he agrees to go through exactly what she went through. It doesn't turn out well.

Gordon Marks killed Bobby Lightfoot. Now they'd find out exactly what happened because Gordon Marks was going to kill them. The circle would be complete.

Movies! Imagination!

Splash.

Heather said, "Did you hear—"

The three of them about-faced. In the creek, on the far side, not far behind them, stood Gordon and Steven Marks. Steven held a hatchet. Gordon made eye contact with her, smiled, and opened a straight razor as he lifted it in his right hand.

"RUN!" Max shouted.

The command had an instant effect. Max took a slight lead, but Heather and Janet stayed on his heels as they bolted downstream, wasting no more time on the potentially crippling sight of the killers behind them, on the image of *children* with weapons in their hands and hunger on their faces.

Splash-splash-splash-splash.

The splashing stopped, which meant the Marks boys were climbing out of the creek onto shore. Janet didn't think she and Heather and Max had enough of a lead to be safe. Where could they go? Where could they hide? The path was straight. The trees on their left were so dense, they were like a wall—

But Max cut left, toward the trees.

The trees would slow them down. Give the hatchet and

razor all the time they needed to—

Max slipped into the trees. Heather followed. Janet followed.

Within the trees, more trees. They could maneuver. Slowly. Janet whispered, "Max! They saw where we went!"

"I hope so," Max said. "In here is the only way we lose them."

Some gaps were wide enough, and some they had to squeeze through, but they managed a winding path through the trees. Janet sensed, somehow, that Max was still leading them downstream.

Enough time passed for Janet to be sure that, if the Marks boys were chasing, they were in the trees now, too. Max must have reached the same conclusion because he led them out of the trees, to a place where a thorny thicket blocked their way to the creek.

Along with buzzing insects, cawing birds, and a kind of... restlessness... nature's sounds distorted, warped... male voices came from the trees. Their pursuers were close.

"We can't keep running," Janet said, wishing she could say something they *could* do. Fight? With what? Numbers and age were on their side, but the Marks boys seemed like a force. Unnatural. Like—

Heather broke away from Janet and Max as she said, "We follow their example and hide on the other side of these bushes until they pass us by." Janet was fast behind her as she led through a space between thickets.

Heather crouched behind a bush, and Janet crouched beside her. Janet looked back, expecting Max. Her head jerked back to Heather when she heard, "What the—ow!"

A vine extending from one of the bushes had wrapped around Heather's right wrist tightly enough for thorns to pierce skin. Janet looked, processing what had happened, and didn't notice the vine curling its way up her left leg until it reached her knee and tightened. Janet cried out as she fell backward, landing hard on her backside as the vine tugged her toward the bush, biting her with its thorns.

As Heather tried to pull her right hand away, another vine wrapped around her left. When her skin broke, she let a tiny scream escape.

A vine was seizing Janet's right forearm when Max appeared at her side and yanked it in the opposite direction, tossing it toward the trees. He leaned over and, with his bare hands, pried the vine away from Janet's leg, loosening it enough for her to scurry away.

Max, with his bare hands, now bloody, freed Heather as well. They all moved away from what would have been their hiding place. Near the creek, they were out in the open. Heather and Janet, bleeding from the thorns' small punctures, got to their feet.

A voice from the trees, male, adolescent, likely Steven: "I heard them! This way!"

Janet, approaching panic, looked at Heather, then at Max. Max wiped his hands on his black jeans. The blood came off. He didn't appear to be bleeding. He had *clutched* the thorny vines when he had freed Janet and Heather.

Why wasn't Max bleeding?

Bobby

"I don't think Thing One and Thing Two would mind getting a little wet," Bobby said, scratching Thing One behind an ear. He wondered how a big uber-dog like Thing One could end up with such a long scar on its nose. Did the creatures of The Middle Reaches fight each other? Maybe. If all the *things* here were on the same side, Sheldon wouldn't have been sent to look after him.

Sheldon shook his head. "No, not here. It's not safe to cross the creek here."

Bobby couldn't doubt Sheldon, but he had to ask: "Why?"

"Fish."

With a smile, Bobby said, "Unless they're like, lionfish, I don't see what's so scary—"

"These fish are scary." Sheldon's head drooped. He probably didn't mean to call attention to his bare feet, but Bobby glanced at them again. The ground was rough in some places and muddy in others. Sheldon's feet had to hurt, but he didn't seem bothered. Bobby didn't want to ask him about it. Another, possibly related, question had wormed its way into his mind, and it threatened to take over.

"Besides," Sheldon said, "The Middle Reaches prepared an alternate route."

Sheldon looked at the fallen tree that kept them from continuing to follow the creek on this side, and then he turned toward the wall of trees, impossibly big trees, *impassably* big trees, with a lower wall of slithering vines in front of them—

except, where Sheldon indicated, Bobby saw an opening. Like the vines had created for him before. A passage. "Don't be surprised," Sheldon said. "I think something wants to show us... something."

Bobby wanted to ask him... *something*. Did it make any sense? Did it make too much sense?

They passed into the crowd of enormous growth, and in seconds they came to a singular group of smaller trees with pale grey bark. The smaller trees formed a circle. Each member of the circle had... *someone*... inside.

"A Grove of Ghosts," Sheldon said. Maybe he'd gotten the

name for the place somewhere else. He crossed through the circle, to a tree where a woman's head and chest, covered in bark like the rest of her, protruded, and one of her legs stepped out. Waves around her head suggested long hair. Sheldon put a hand on her torn, miserable face and said, "Celia."

Bobby recognized someone, too. Lying on a tree, halfway sunken in, Chris also looked torn. *Flayed*. The word was *flayed*. The contours of his bare chest were sculpted in bark, but swaths of skin were obviously missing, and elsewhere were gashes. Someone had cut him. Someone had cut him everywhere.

Someone had killed him.

Gordon Marks. Which led him back to the worm in his brain—but instead he asked, "Why? Why am I supposed to see this? Why am I supposed to know? *What* am I supposed to know?"

"I wish I could tell you," Sheldon said. "I've never... been here... and I'm not inclined to stay." He walked toward another part of the circle. "There's a way out, too."

He led toward an opening between two trees, each of which held a person in agony, body mangled but mercifully unfamiliar. Bobby followed, Things One and Two at his sides, and a short trail led them back to the enormous trees and then to a view of the creek.

Or what remained of the creek—it was even smaller now than it was in Steven's backyard. It flowed into an overgrowth of roots and vines that masked a mound of stone jutting from the earth. Without pause, Sheldon moved toward the mound. Bobby followed.

When they got close, the roots and vines parted. "This is it," Sheldon said. "A little sooner than expected. The Cavern of The Mouth."

"A door," Bobby said. "Another door. Why do doors keep opening for me?" That wasn't the question. *Ask the question!*

"There's no denying that you're a special kind of guy," Sheldon said with a slanted but—affectionate?—grin. Sheldon was charming. Sheldon was handsome. Maybe if Bobby could be with Sheldon, the answer to his question wouldn't matter.

"Sheldon," Bobby said, working up his nerve, "am I...."

"Yes, you are. Very special indeed."

"No, what I mean to ask is... am I... dead?" The question sounded so ludicrous!

Sheldon's grin faded. "Well if you are, I am," Sheldon said.

Bobby felt lightheaded. "That's not an answer."

Sheldon said, "What do you think?"

Memory flashes, Gordon tying him to a tree and calling him ugly, Gordon and the sounds of his own bones breaking. "I think Gordon Marks killed me."

"Yeah," Sheldon said. "I don't know who Gordon Marks is, but yeah." He put a hand on Bobby's shoulder. "You and me, we've got being dead in common, too." He pulled Bobby closer.

"I thought... it didn't make sense... but nothing here does, so...."

Sheldon hugged him and said, "Are you okay?"

"Yeah," Bobby said, about to cry and fighting it. "I already knew. It's okay." Being so close to Sheldon made his heart's tempo skyrocket.

Sheldon held the hug for what seemed like a long time before he pushed them apart and said, "Okay then. The only way to go is forward. Which is more terrifying, hope or despair?"

What a crazy question! Unless it was a trick question? "Despair, I think," Bobby said.

"I think so, too. Let's keep going." Sheldon led, and Bobby, dead but not crying about it, followed him inside the Cavern of The Mouth.

Heather

She and Janet were barely on their feet when Steven— older but recognizable—came out of the trees, hatchet in hand. The taller boy behind him had to be Gordon. She'd known with certainty as soon as she'd seen them, and she'd known to run, but now they were so close, and she didn't know what to do.

Janet said, "Now is probably a bad time to mention that Steven held his school's records for sprinting and cross-country. And Gordon just looks fast."

The armed set of two stood in front of the trees, watching the unarmed set of three who stood in front of the creek. Nobody flinched.

"We should be running anyway," Max said.

"Right," Heather said, not moving and afraid to breathe. The thorny vines had *grabbed* her. On their own they had *taken hold* of her. And now a psycho with a razor and a psycho with a hatchet

psychos she'd wanted to feel closer to—

were close enough to—

No. Fuck that. "When I say go," she said, "we—"

A voice, a thundering whisper, surrounded them: "*HURRY.*"

That was good enough for Heather. "Go!"

They ran downstream, Heather taking the lead. She looked behind her as she advanced, making sure Max and Janet were in step, confirming that the psycho brothers were in pursuit, and she faced forward again as Janet halted and screamed, "HEATHER, NO!"

Being scolded like a dog had no meaning at first, but as her eyes registered the figure in front of her—broad-shouldered and otherwise shaped like a man, but also like an inkblot, filled with darkness, collecting darkness, shimmering darkness—she understood that "no" meant "stop," and she tried to stop and did only as she collided with the man made of shadow.

The Shadow Man, her mind told her, as part of her slipped into the dark.

She saw a man in front of her, or a man broken down into puzzle pieces, limbs and head and chest and middle bloodily divided but held in suspension, related parts detached but adjacent. The visual image fled quickly, overwhelmed by freezing cold and a feeling of being utterly bereft, sadness of a depth she had never known, sadness that felt like an infinity of infinities. It turned her into glass. Heather felt like she was made of glass.

"*This is not your time*," the whispering boomed. Heather backed away, separating from the freezing infinities. Not her time for what?

She turned around. For a second, she saw Gordon and Steven, ready to attack. A second later, they were gone. Vanished. As if someone had flipped a switch and shut them off.

It was not *their* time.

"*Hurry*," The Shadow Man repeated. Max approached him.

"We have to do what he says," Heather said. The Shadow Man beckoned, and she felt his call with every part of her. They would hurry. They would go where the creek led.

"Are you CRAZY?" Janet yelled.

Max

Max placed his hand on—or over, because it wasn't solid—The Shadow Man's shoulder.

"Are you CRAZY?" Janet yelled.

Max understood that The Shadow Man, or most of him, had had a name and a life and memories, all of which taunted him now. Would more of Max's memories return to him? Did he even want them to? Max had been someone, and now he was a shadow of that someone.

The Shadow Man had power, but it was not *his* power. He performed, playing puppet to whatever gave Max his *purpose*, too.

The Shadow Man radiated intense loneliness, a loneliness Max understood because he had no one, and though he felt yearning for Heather, he didn't think she'd return it, and the yearning wasn't even his. It was The Middle Reaches working through him. He was a scooped-out void. He and The Shadow Man had that in common. Void. Overwhelming coldness, a nothing inside.

The Shadow Man wasn't his shadow. He was his reflection.

Sheldon

The wall of roots and vines that blocked the corridor opened immediately, and Sheldon imagined Bobby's experience of seeing it all for the first time, the swirling clouds, purple, red, pink, and white, with dots of black reminiscent of the Inner Layers' black stars—and presumably the stars in Carcosa's sky as well. The Gate condensed the majesty of The Middle Reaches into a single spot.

Sheldon gestured for Bobby to move along, but he didn't feel as confident as he had. Ushering Nick to The Watcher had been a condemnation. He'd known the likely outcome, at least vaguely, and he had abetted it. He'd taken part in Leslie's death, too, though in that circumstance he'd had less control. But if The Watcher had taken her like it had taken Nick, Sheldon's complicity would have been the same.

He didn't want to be complicit in The Watcher showing Bobby a fate worse than death. He rather liked the boy—liked spending time with him—liked how quickly he caught on to ideas—liked how much they had in common. They could turn around. Sheldon didn't have to encourage Bobby to let The Watcher *assess* him. He didn't have to let The Mouth tear him apart.

But going through The Mouth was the only way to go through the Gate.

Without encouragement, Bobby moved through the opening in the wall. Sheldon stayed close. Thing One and Thing Two came behind. In the swirling clouds, The Watcher's greyish form turned. It anticipated them. Sheldon felt its yearning, a powerful hook in his chest. Bobby must have felt it, too. He continued forward. Sheldon didn't know if he could stop the boy, but he would stay by his side. They might both be destroyed.

Or Sheldon might go with him, if Bobby passed through.

As Bobby and Sheldon got closer, rows of teeth, top and bottom, became visible. They swirled nearer, then farther.

"The Mouth," Bobby said.

"Yes." Around them, the walls screamed.

"And I'm facing some kind of trial," Bobby said. "If I fail, this thing tears me to pieces."

"Yes." Sheldon had been honest. He hadn't told Bobby to run, and maybe he should have, but he had told Bobby the truth.

Together with the screams from the walls: *shhh, shhh, shhh, shhh, shhh, shhh, shhh, shhh.*

Bobby shrugged. "I guess it doesn't matter. I'm already dead, right?"

The boy moved into the swirling clouds. Sheldon wanted to shout "Wait!," to grab him, to explain that so much worse could happen, to take him out of here, to a safety away from The

Middle Reaches, if that were even possible, but instead, all he could do was keep up, staying by the kid's side.

In front of them, the rows of teeth reappeared, and this time, they stayed in place. Upper teeth, lower teeth, and in the middle—

At the sides, eddies formed in the clouds. Slender tongues, squirming like tentacles, extended, but they didn't latch on to either of them. The tentacle-tongues wavered at the boys' sides, and—

And in the middle, where The Mouth gaped open—

A passage.

EPISODE 22:
FARTHER REACHES

Janet

"Are you CRAZY?" Janet yelled. She didn't know who was crazier, Heather or Max. Heather had rushed headlong into the shadow... man... thing... and now Max was... touching it... him... if touching a shape of inky blackness were possible—

Heather said *to do what he says*. Bonkers.

Janet looked from "him" to the place where the Marks boys had been with their hatchet and razor. She'd been looking right at them when they'd disappeared. She hadn't blinked. They'd simply stopped being.

A light breeze hit her from behind. She turned.

"He" was gone, too. No more shimmering shadow-shape. Heather, Max, and Janet. Alone again with the creek, which babbled along with the caws, the buzzes, and the other noises surrounding them that sounded less and less natural under the cloudless white-grey sky.

Alone again with Heather. She thought about what they could do, alone, with no one to see... except Max. Goddamned Max.

Janet thought instead about her bleeding leg and looked down. Most of the places where the thorns had dug in had stopped oozing, but a few still trickled. Thorns. On vines. That moved on their own.

"Did you feel that?" Max asked Heather.

"Cold," Heather said. "As he... left, a blast of freezing cold."

They sounded calm. Pensive. Absurd. "What—the—*hell?*" Janet said, stepping closer to them. "We've got ghostly shadow people bellowing about time, psycho-killers running after us who vanish into thin air, and vines that move around with minds of their own, and you're commenting on the *temperature?*"

Heather looked toward the spot where the Marks boys had disappeared, and with wide eyes, she shook her head. "When I know what to say about... *that*... I'll say it." Heather was composed. Rational. Irresistible. Her wrists were bleeding.

"I think The Shadow Man helped us," Max said.

"'The Shadow Man,'" Janet repeated, mimicking Max's tone of voice. "That's, like, his name? I assume you two are intimately acquainted." Max, intimate. He probably wanted Heather. And Janet had seen the way Heather looked at him.

"No," Max said. "I've never seen him before. I have no idea about this place... unnatural... supernatural...."

Heather said, "When I touched him, I felt him. I felt...."

"Yeah," Max said.

They were bonding over touching some kind of supernatural monster! "Max," Janet said, straightening her back. "Show us your hands."

"What?" Max said.

"Show us your damned hands!"

Max held out his hands, palms down. "What do you want with—"

Janet grabbed his hands and turned them over, positioning them in front of Heather. "See?" she said.

"He has nice hands," Heather said, giving Janet a sideways glare.

"No!" Janet shouted, considering that maybe she was confusing too many issues, vines, psycho-killers, The Shadow Man, and—"He's not bleeding!"

"You were expecting stigmata?" Heather said.

Heather had an admirable wit, even though she used it at Janet's expense. Janet took a breath. The air filled her with tingling. "No," she said, calmer. "He pried those vines off us with his bare hands. I'm bleeding. You're bleeding. He should be, too."

A tense moment passed while Heather looked from Janet to Max and back again, but then Heather edged closer to Janet and said, "Max, she has a point. Can you explain your failure to bleed?"

Max looked at his palms. "Lucky, I guess?"

"You guess," Janet grumbled.

"What should we do?" Heather looked at Janet.

"Me?" Janet asked. She realized she didn't know what she wanted to do, but she knew the logical answer: "We get the hell out of here. Forget about this place. Pretend it was a bad dream."

Heather looked from Janet to Max and back again. She took a deep breath. "You smell that? I'm pretty sure it's... honeysuckle. So sweet. Mouth-watering. Exhilarating."

"Honeysuckle," Janet said, taking a deep breath, "and rot." But it *was* exhilarating. It made her want more.

Heather pressed close, so close their chests touched, and she kissed Janet on the forehead. "Going back might be just as dangerous as going forward, and I'm not ready to give up on what might lie ahead." Heather moved to Max and placed a hand on his cheek. "I know *you* agree with me."

"Yeah," Max said, shifting from foot to foot. He had a bulge in his pants. "We follow the creek."

"What about *you*?" Heather asked Janet. "Are you turning back, or are you coming with us?"

"I won't let you go alone!" Janet blurted. She blushed. The place on her forehead where Heather had kissed her tingled most, but other parts of her, parts that wanted to touch and be touched, felt charged with static electricity. "I mean," she said, "I want to know. I never want to come back here, but since we're here... we have to find out, don't we? What it's about?"

Whether they were inhaling hallucinogenic mushroom spores or really facing supernatural forces?

Whether Heather might decide to kiss her again?

Gordon

Goddamn shit fucking hell—

"Gordon?" Steven, with a question on the tip of his tongue.

"WHAT?"

One voice said "shhh." Another screamed.

"Where are we?" Steven asked. He sounded so much younger than he was supposed to be.

They walked on a downward slope through what seemed like hallways cut unevenly through rock, a cave made on purpose, with vines and roots clinging to the walls, tendrils that, the deeper they got, tended more and more to reach for them. A purplish glow lit their way through mist, but ahead of them was brighter and whiter. What lay ahead had its own light.

"The Cavern of The Mouth," Gordon answered. He wanted to add, *Don't ask questions*, but he had no reason because he was full of questions, so he couldn't blame Steven for having them, too. The problem was that he didn't give a shit where they were because he was still pissed off they weren't where they'd been.

He wanted to know what the straight razor, still in his hand, felt like when it split a girl's skin.

Why had they blacked out when their prey, their purpose, had been so close?

What was that thing, that man, made out of darkness?

"I thought that's where we were," Steven said.

The rough hallway turned, and the light became even brighter. Not too far ahead, vines and roots stretched down from the walls and ceiling and formed a wall, but it had an opening in it, and light shined through the opening, flickering light, still purple, but also red and pink and white. The Inner Layers, the Middle Layers, the First Layers, the Border, skies, frontiers, all swirling.

You can see the timeless clockwork. The Watcher. The Mouth. The Gate. The voice Gordon heard sounded like Adam, and it sounded inhuman.

He heard other voices, too. Ahead of them. He couldn't make out what they were saying, so he advanced. Steven stayed at his side.

As they approached the opening in the wall, the voices became clearer.

"I'm facing some kind of trial. If I fail, this thing tears me to pieces."

"Bobby?" Steven asked, excited, speeding the rest of the way toward the wall.

Gordon caught him before he could go through the opening, turned him so they'd face each other. Gordon said, "Shhh."

A voice on the other side of the wall, one he didn't recognize, said, "Yes."

The hallway didn't echo, but it responded to Gordon: "Shhh, shhh, shhh, shhh, shhh, shhh, shhh, shhh."

83

Through the opening, Gordon could see that one of the two boys standing in front of the swirl of multicolored clouds, the older boy, was unfamiliar, but the other was indeed Bobby Lightfoot. Gordon looked at his razor. Killing that kid had opened new worlds for him, but what was the point of killing someone if he showed up again as if nothing ever—

The dead have purpose here, too.

Maybe Bobby's purpose was to get killed by Gordon a second time? The idea amused him. Gordon could go on killing Bobby, forever. The expression on Steven's face, though —eyes tearing up simply seeing the kid again—made him think otherwise. He knew Steven and Bobby had done stuff that made him want to puke, but he didn't care like he used to. The volume on perversity had been turned down pretty low.

"I guess it doesn't matter," Bobby said. "I'm already dead, right?"

Besides, between where Bobby stood with the bigger kid and where Gordon stood watching with Steven were two giant dog-like creatures, creatures that didn't look like they'd be too friendly to anybody intruding on Bobby and the other kid.

"Gordon," Steven whispered, barely audible. "Do you understand what's happening?"

"Just watch," Gordon said, matching his brother's volume.

They watched through the opening in the wall. Bobby and the bigger kid moved into the swirling clouds, and as they did, rows of teeth appeared, arcs of fangs, above them and below them, The Mouth. Bobby and the bigger kid walked *inside The Mouth.*

And disappeared.

As the dog-creatures followed them, Steven jumped through the opening in the wall, screaming, "WAIT!" He started for the swirling clouds.

Gordon lunged through the opening for a tackle, knowing that if he merely ran, Steven could get away. The boys connected, going down on the uneven stone ground. Gordon raised his head and saw his brother raising his head, looking toward where The Mouth had been—and wasn't now. Only swirls of color, dotted with black.

Soft sounds, close enough to be heard along with the screaming from the walls. Steven was crying. "I wish you hadn't," he said. "I wish you hadn't told me what you did to him."

Heather

The creek continued straight in the direction where they were walking, but also, on the other side, beyond a stretch of grassy land, the creek seemed to rise out of nowhere and flow into a place where the sky turned pink. Heather stopped, got the others' attentions, and said, "It's a fork."

Max gazed up toward the pink sky. Janet glanced at the deviant part of the creek and gave Heather a quizzical frown.

"We need to cross," Max said.

"Oh, *screw* that," Janet said. "The way we're going is fine."

"It's the wrong way," Max said.

"The water has to be up to our waists, or higher," Janet said.

Max was still looking at the pink sky, which made Heather think about it. "If the first rule is, follow the creek," Heather said, unsure of when that had become a rule, "the second rule seems to be, follow the weird." Heather paused, waiting for Janet to respond. When Janet stayed silent, Heather explained, "The sky over there is pink. I think it's a sign we should cross and go that way."

"Why are you taking *his* side?" Janet asked.

"I didn't know we were on sides," Heather said. "But if it's a democracy...."

"Fine," Janet said. Janet marched to the creek, took graceful steps halfway down the bank, and hopped into the water. Without looking back, she continued toward the other side.

"Okay, then," Heather said, not sure whether she should be glad the fight hadn't been as hard as she'd expected, not sure how mad Janet might be, not sure that venturing toward an even more unnatural sky was really a good idea. She joined Janet in the water, and Max came close behind.

The farther they got, the stronger the current got, making waist-high water crash against them and soak their shirts. The water felt warm, almost pleasant. It soothed the cuts on Heather's wrists.

Without incident, Janet arrived at the other side, and she gave Heather a hand up. Janet took several backward steps away from the creek, her eyes having obvious trouble staying away from the places where Heather's t-shirt clung to her chest. Janet's shirt clung, too. Heather could see her nipples. She could touch them if she wanted. Janet wanted her. Heather knew. She'd always known.

They shared a moment of knowing while Heather heard Max lift himself from water to shore.

Janet touched Heather's hair, stroking it behind her ear.

Heather turned her head toward Max. He took off his shirt and wrung it, pouring water near his shoes. His body was young but not unformed, with broad shoulders, ripples for biceps and triceps, defined pecs, and a few hairs sticking to the center of a moisture-beaded chest that was almost as tan as his face and arms. His flat stomach had a trail of hair leading from his bellybutton down into the wet jeans that hung loosely from his hips.

Janet's head turned toward him, and for a moment, Heather thought she might be interested, too. "You would find a reason to take your shirt off," Janet said.

"It was soaked," Max said, approaching them, shirt in hand. "I thought I could—"

Janet looked at Max's crotch and said, "Yeah, I know what you're thinking."

Heather inhaled as deeply as she could, letting the tingling flow to her extremities and strobe in her brain. "You know what I'm thinking?" she said.

Max and Janet looked at her. Janet's lips parted, but she didn't say anything.

Heather kissed the parted lips, giving the upper one a teasing lick. Janet looked stunned. "I'm thinking," Heather said, "we should all get out of these wet clothes."

She kissed Max, opening his mouth for him, while she placed a hand on his bare chest and slid it down, over his flat stomach, past the waistline of his jeans, down, down—

Steven

"WAIT!" he screamed, and he darted through the door in the wall. He didn't understand The Mouth, or the Gate, or what Bobby and that older boy disappearing in the swirling color clouds meant, but if he could see Bobby up close, talk to him one more time, touch his hand, it might—

It might make up for what he had become. His mind didn't articulate the thought, not in words, but it was there, a part of him, driving him.

A second later, his teeth smashed together as his chin hit rock. The tackle was swift but not hard. Gordon had brought him down to stop him, not to hurt him, even though the whole front of his body shrieked at the impact. Gordon, who had killed

Bobby months before he killed Chris.

Gordon, who had told Steven, tied up in a corner, *how* he killed Bobby *while* he killed Chris. Gordon cut Chris again and again and sliced off skin like patches of fabric and then, as Chris died, talked about beating Bobby with a shovel and then cutting him, too, *castrating* him, and Steven couldn't turn off his ears. He had to listen. He listened, and he saw it in his head.

Steven was crying. "I wish you hadn't," he said. "I wish you hadn't told me what you did to him."

He and his brother rearranged themselves so they sat facing each other, the swirling clouds behind Steven, the colorful light shining on Gordon's face, which grinned. "I made you the man you are today," Gordon said.

"We," Steven said, and he stopped. When had Gordon ever taken one of *his* suggestions? His heart beat faster, gathering the momentum to push words out of his mouth with enough volume to overcome all the noises of this... Cavern. "We need to go after Bobby."

"Through the Gate," Gordon said. He might have been listening to something. He picked up the straight razor, which he must have dropped during the tackle, and wiped the blade on his pants leg as if it were a strop. "I wouldn't mind seeing Bobby again."

"NO!" Steven shouted. He'd kept the hatchet in his hand, and after he shouted, he noticed he'd raised it.

Gordon asked, "What are you going to do with that, Stevie?"

Steven lowered the hatchet—but only halfway. "You're not going to hurt any of my friends again."

Gordon chuckled. "You don't have any friends. I'm your only friend."

Rising fury made his ears burn. "YOU'RE NOT GOING TO

HURT BOBBY EVER AGAIN!"

"Bobby's already dead, Steven," Gordon said, still grinning.

"Say it!" Steven demanded, feeling strong, feeling—*right.*

"Say what?"

"Say you're not—"

"Okay, okay," Gordon said. "I'm not going to hurt your friend Bobby ever again."

Steven wasn't sure he believed Gordon, but he felt glad to hear him say it.

Max

He might have been dead, but he was also one of the luckiest guys on the planet.

Granted, he wouldn't have made any promises about what planet they were on, but he didn't really care with the soft grass beneath his bare side and a naked girl pressing in front of and behind him. His mouth connected with Heather's mouth, then Janet's, and then the girls' mouths connected. Janet's fingers guided and joined Max's cock as it slid inside Heather again, into almost unbearable wetness and heat.

Envelopes enveloped him with pleasure. If he could disappear this way, he'd volunteer.

Some guys thought about baseball to stave off the climax, the unwanted end. Instead, Max thought about being dead. Because Janet was right. Not that she seemed to mind at the moment, but he *should* have bled from handling those vines. He'd felt the thorns prick him. He wasn't immune to pain... or pleasure... and people obviously responded to his touch... but he had some exemption from injury.

He was, in some ways, corporeal, but, in other ways, he

was... not. He moved according to drives he didn't comprehend and carried only fragments of memories of a life that felt separate from himself.

Was he... a ghost?

A ghost fucking his ectoplasmic brains out with two slightly older teenage girls?

Janet wrapped a long leg around both him and Heather, kissed the back of his head, then leaned in for a deeper kiss with Heather that nudged Max's mouth aside. Max understood Janet's priorities. He hadn't really understood before they were all naked, but Janet's facial expression as she examined Max's and Heather's bodies side by side said that she'd be nice to Max, but she only truly wanted Heather.

When they'd started, Heather had gone down on Max, and Janet had gone down on Heather. That left Max's mouth for Janet, and he didn't mind. Impressions of memories—Annie teaching him do's and don'ts of cunnilingus—guided him. Even though it was in the wrong category of mouth for the girl whose thighs wrapped around his ears, he could still use his tongue to rock Janet's world.

Dead. He was dead, a ghost, but not merely a ghost. He felt tethered to this place, The Middle Reaches. It, or they, or something within them, gave him purpose. He left the field to increase the flock. He shepherded Heather and Janet toward home.

Who cares when a shepherd lies down with his sheep?

The thought made him pause. It almost deflated the moment as Max's mind drifted into bestial images, but Janet called him back by crawling over him, practically rolling over Heather, and situating herself on Heather's other side. Heather was in an envelope now, and Max thrust into her harder, staring into her eyes as Janet's hands slipped in front of him to knead Heather's breasts.

A shepherd-ghost. A shepherd-ghost who had died... he felt the scooped-out sensation in his stomach... horribly... but who now served... a shepherd-god. *Hastur.* An unfamiliar voice whispered the name in his head. A powerful god. *Hastur.*

His enjoyment of Heather and Janet was a gift from Hastur.

Max didn't feel certain about anything. He had seen enough about himself when he touched The Shadow Man to accept some... intuitions... as bankable truths. But mostly, he felt uncertain.

When he climaxed, would he ejaculate? Was he the kind of ghost with no bodily fluids at all?

Bobby

Bobby felt like the static that's on TV when you disconnect the cable. He was incoherent, inchoate, a war of splotches with no objectives. The dissipation elated, uplifted, tickled his lips and inflated his lungs with cool air. A breeze teased his skin as he faced forward, into it, and advanced.

White light exploded like a flashbulb. The surroundings settled into green. Green light shone from behind him. He cast a long shadow on the ground in front of him. The shadow touched a wall.

His shadow made from green light didn't stand alone. Beside it stood another long shadow

Sheldon's! Sheldon stood beside him, and the Gate, now green, was behind them. Which meant—

"We," Bobby said, "we lived through it."

"I wouldn't count on this meaning we're *alive*," Sheldon said. He stood close enough to hold Bobby's hand. He probably would if Bobby asked him to. Bobby didn't think he'd be bothered. Sheldon seemed like he did whatever Sheldon wanted to do, no matter what people thought, and Bobby admired him. Bobby wouldn't impose on Sheldon now, but he felt glad that—whatever—had sent him.

The wall in front of them was made of live worms, brown and white and black. It blocked their passage across a bridge over a vast green nothing. The worms would disperse soon, showing the way. Bobby could be patient. He was meant to see Carcosa. He understood. He'd been chosen.

EPISODE 23: LOST CARCOSA

Sheldon

They burrow, they slide through.

They know how to hide, too!

They break into pieces,

And that's how one becomes a few.

They know where the feast is:

They're headed there, inside of you!

Worms.

Platyhelminths, nematodes, annelids.

Worms.

Sheldon had discussed the wriggling, repugnant, often parasitic creatures with the Cavern. He hadn't known why. Perhaps the wall explained.

The wall that blocked entrance to, and even a fair glimpse of, Carcosa.

"Bobby, don't," Sheldon said as the boy moved closer to the wall. To the worms. Sheldon would have rather done anything than get closer to the worms.

"It's okay," Bobby said. He stood at the wall, raised a hand, and pressed his palm close to it. Sheldon's stomach turned as the worms welcomed the hand, sliding over it. "It's okay," Bobby repeated.

The wall melted. Worms, wriggling together, writhing together, disbanded, and the wall lost integrity, settling into a mound, dripping worms over the edges of the—bridge—where they stood, dripping them over into a green void.

Bobby stood still as the worms moved away from him. *Why do doors keep opening for me?*

A special kind of guy.

The view distracted Sheldon from considering how well Bobby understood his specialness. He saw the shoreline and the lake moving along it, stroking it with waves because Lake Hali was enormous, and the influence of the two moons—

The sky! No, *not* two moons, but three, at least three that Sheldon could see now. They didn't look like the bruises that hung over The Middle Reaches on the other side of the Gate but like jewel-encrusted, circular plateaus in the air, one shining with emerald, one with amethyst, and one with aquamarine.

The sky that held them lacked continuous color. It was a collection of brushstrokes, primary and secondary shades shifting in relation to each other like slow blood cells traveling through invisible, wandering arteries.

In front of the brushstrokes, black stars shimmered. They were bigger and *closer* than before. They provided light beyond the visible spectrum. They provided a *hum*.

Sheldon reasoned that the bridge where they stood was still The Middle Reaches. As the worm-wall reduced to nothing, he saw that the bridge continued, and it met more bridges.

But Lake Hali! Its shores lapped by water, if the liquid spilling onto the squiggly cobalt-blue land actually was water, capped by eddying mists, mists that seemed more... deliberate... than the mists that hung without purpose on the other side of the Gate. Were the mists alive? Was the *lake* alive? What did the

God of the Lake choose to animate?

The creatures of The Middle Reaches served different masters, but almost all of them spawned in the realm of Lake Hali.

Running along the shore of Lake Hali, a white, magnificent wall reached toward the black stars and the brushstrokes. It had high crenellated ramparts but lacked visible signs of masonry or other construction. This feature, too, Sheldon had discussed with the Cavern. The wall of the Walled City was not built. The God of the Palace, the King in Yellow, Hastur, had grown in it from the bones of captives.

The wall was mostly human, bone reinforced by sacrifice, white as pure opal, harder than diamond.

Sheldon couldn't see the part of the wall with the entrance, The Glass Citadel, though its multicolored spires did stand out above the wall. Between where he and Bobby stood and where the entrance must have been stretched a bleak and desolate expanse of plain—part of Lost Carcosa—the Old City—through which they would cross.

The bridge led there. The bridge led away from the green void, which land and liquid soon replaced, and split into or joined with other bridges, disappearing into the mists of Lake Hali or providing paths into Lost Carcosa or toward and around the Walled City. The bridges, suspended in the air by inhuman engineering, connected to outlets in void space like the one emitting green light behind them.

There were likely other Gates. Other Middle Reaches? Other places where ceaseless yearning brought people... or *others*... here?

Hum. The stars' vibration rattled Sheldon's chest, making him more aware of his heartbeat. Strange to be dead and to have a heartbeat. Yet looking out at Lake Hali, the Walled City, the Lost City, and the network of connections that formed this side

95

of The Middle Reaches, he'd never felt so alive.

Gordon

Gordon's promises didn't mean shit. Steven knew that, and Steven wanted to follow his friend Bobby and that other kid through the Gate, and that was fine with him. He still hadn't shaken off being mad about turning up here in the first place, the Cavern of The Mouth, when he'd been after—

Her. And *her*. And that dipshit Max Gracey. *Again*.

But maybe seeing the other side of this Gate wouldn't be so bad. Bobby had said something about knowing he was dead. That was pretty trippy. Gordon didn't think you had to be dead, though, to go through the Gate and be okay. He and Steven weren't dead. They were messed up somehow, but they weren't dead. They'd be fine, though, walking into those swirling clouds. He felt sure.

He didn't know why.

Gordon squeezed the razor's polished handle in his right hand while he stood, eyes on the swirling clouds. He didn't see The Mouth. He didn't see the giant grey form. "We going?" he asked.

Steven looked up at him, perplexed. "Going?"

"You want to follow Bobby, right?" Gordon didn't mention the dog-like creatures. He didn't want to, but they could deal with Bobby's pets if they had to. He felt sure.

Steven stood and faced the clouds. "Let's go."

Gordon thought about counting down to a charge but felt stupid, so he walked forward until the light blinded him. Steven stayed close to his side. He sensed his brother there until—

Blackout.

When vision came back into focus, Gordon saw a bush,

like the bushes they had hidden behind before but bigger, with thicker vines and longer thorns. He looked up: pink sky, white not too far off. They were at the edge of the First Layers. Not far from where—

He didn't know whether to laugh or scream in frustration. "Fuck," he whispered. He stifled a laugh when he realized how appropriate the word was. Still—they had gone through the Gate and ended up *here?*

"What?" Steven said at full volume.

"Shhh!" Gordon said, one hand on Steven to keep him from exposing their vantage. With the other hand, he pointed at the show.

Max, Bobby's old babysitter, and the other girl were naked and rolling around in the grass, doing it. Gordon could see tits and asses, and he knew from the way Max moved that Max was inside the babysitter, and Gordon was rock-hard, rubbing the straight razor's smooth handle.

"Enough frustration," Gordon whispered through clenched teeth. "Let's finish what we started."

Steven looked at the hatchet in his hand, looked at Gordon, looked at the three fuckers in the grass, looked back at Gordon, and nodded.

"Wait for my signal, then run at them," Gordon said. Not yet. No, not yet. He wanted to watch a while.

Max

When he came—he *felt* like he came—he thrusted deep inside of Heather, who tilted her head back, making Janet's face visible behind her, and Heather moaned like she was climaxing, too. Annie never would have let Max come inside her. But he was probably dead, right? Dead guys don't get girls pregnant. They don't have diseases, either.

The sensation of pulling out made him want to howl. He collapsed on his back and lay on the grass, his vision spotty.

Luckiest guy on the planet.

Heather rolled to her other side, away from Max, toward Janet. Seconds later, Janet was grunting. The sound was almost a squeal—a little off-putting, but kind of cute, too. Before long Janet was almost screaming, and in his head, Max saw Heather's fingers down where his tongue had been, saw Janet finally getting what she wanted, and when Janet's noise reached a peak, he felt her orgasm like an aftershock of his own. He rode her long sigh downward...

What was—?

Distraction. He must have lain on a rock or something. It poked between his shoulder blades.

They all lay on their backs, Heather in the middle, fidgeting with Max's nearby hand—and, he assumed, with Janet's nearby hand—with playful fingers. Insects buzzed. Birds cawed. Trees and bushes rustled with sourceless movements. Above, in one direction, Max saw white sky, and in the other, he saw pink. They were supposed to move on, under the pink, in the creek's new direction.

Hastur gave him purpose.

Heather giggled. Nothing else mattered.

"Ow," Heather said, and she giggled again.

"Ow?" Janet said. "Ow," she repeated. "What was that?"

Max felt two pokes in his back, one much lower than the first. "Ow," he whispered, not sure he wanted the girls to hear.

Heather said, "What was—ow!" She lifted the arm near Max. Not far from where thorns had pierced her wrist, a tiny dot of blood bubbled on her forearm.

"Something... prickly?" Janet said. "Something biting us?" Janet sat up. "Oh! That's worse! On my legs and my—"

Janet twisted around to look behind her, giving Heather and Max a view of her back. Heather gasped, sitting up. Max sat up with her. He didn't care about the prickling, now everywhere his body touched the ground, but he cared about Heather, and he even cared about—

"Janet!" Heather cried. "Your back! Everybody, move!"

Heather stood, helping Janet up as she did. Dots of blood, pinpricks, covered both girls' backs, butts, legs, and calves. When they got to their feet, they danced, feet reacting to the sharpness below them, until they moved away from the grass to a bare, muddier area closer to the creek.

The blades of grass where they'd... been together... stood impossibly straight, their tips long and thin, almost invisible, like needles. Max rose and hurried to where the girls watched him. The three, together, naked, gawked at the bed of needles where they'd just had sex.

Janet said, "What...?"

Heather reached behind her, rubbed her lower back, and brought back a bloody palm. "Max?" she said. "Turn around."

"Me?" Max said. It was all he could think of to say.

Janet's eyes widened, taking him in. Heather's inquisitive eyes narrowed. "Yes, you," Heather said.

Max turned in a full circle, not slowing for them to examine his back but knowing what they would see anyway. When he faced them again, he tried his most sympathetic expression.

"You're not bleeding," Heather said.

"What *are* you?" Janet asked.

At a loss for words, he reached for Heather. She stepped away.

Bobby

Sheldon followed Bobby across the area where the worm-wall had been. He caught up without much delay, Thing One and Thing Two trailing behind, but he didn't take the lead. He and Bobby walked together, guided by what Bobby felt was the same sense of direction. Not having Sheldon in charge made Bobby's stomach twist.

They crossed a blighted plain covered with withered grass. A few bare, decaying trees stood apart from each other, but nothing seemed to live. When the wind blew, the grass whistled. The lonely sound might have been worse than all the shrieks and screams on the other side of the Gate. "You haven't been here before," Bobby said.

"No," Sheldon said. "I thought I told you that."

Bobby nodded. "You did. I'm just used to you knowing everything."

Sheldon smiled at him. "I still know things."

"This place?" Bobby said. "I feel like I'm walking through walls, but there's nothing."

"It doesn't look like much, but it's a city, the Old City, the Lost City. Lost Carcosa. We're walking where walls used to be," Sheldon said.

"Ghost walls," Bobby said. "We're ghosts walking through ghost walls," Bobby said.

Sheldon nodded.

They continued in silence until they came upon moss-covered stones with deliberate shapes, some leaning, some lying on the ground, most broken—headstones. Further on, larger blocks might have marked tombs or more important monuments. An abandoned, neglected, ancient graveyard.

"What did it?" Bobby asked. "What killed the city?"

"I'm not sure entirely. I think it was a battleground. Old gods, old grudges," Sheldon said. "There's faded writing carved into some of these stones. It's not any language, or any alphabet, I recognize."

"Me neither," Bobby said. He had seen Egyptian, Aramaic, Sanskrit, Hebrew, Arabic, Chinese... couldn't read them, but could recognize them. These dots, squiggles, and slashes didn't belong to any people Bobby knew about.

"There's something," Sheldon said.

Bobby looked where Sheldon pointed. A short distance away, a man's head, with a nest of knotted black hair on top and a long, ragged beard, seemed to rise from the ground. He was walking up a slope, and soon his whole body came into view. He used a tall crook for a walking stick. He wore a yellow robe over a white tunic and pants cinched at the waist with rope.

"Hello!" Sheldon shouted.

Bobby wasn't sure approaching the bearded man would be a good idea, but Sheldon set out for him, doubling his pace, leading again, so Bobby followed.

"Hello," Sheldon repeated as they got close.

The bearded man held out his crook, halting their advance. "Whom do you serve?"

Thing One and Thing Two growled. The bearded man did not seem impressed.

"You," Sheldon said. "You look like a shepherd. Are you loyal to Hastur?"

The wind blew, surrounding them with the lonely whistling, and the bearded man looked over both of his shoulders. "Hastur does not come here," the man said. "Hastur is not welcome." The man lowered his crook and leaned toward Sheldon confidentially. "I am a man with two masters."

"I understand," Sheldon said. He said it as if *he* had two masters. Did Bobby have even one? He thought of the alternative to Hastur he knew most about, the God of the Citadel, whose avatar was the man in the red shirt, who enjoyed killing people for its own sake.

"Hastur is corrupt," the bearded man, the shepherd, said.

"How?" Sheldon asked.

"Hastur is corruption," the shepherd said.

"What does Hastur *do?*" Bobby asked.

"Child," the shepherd said, addressing Bobby, "yet not a child, Hastur leeches spirit, that within you that makes you."

"I don't understand," Bobby said. What the shepherd said could mean too many things.

"There is that within you that makes a choice, and in choosing makes yourself," the shepherd said. "Hastur consumes it, and you become part of his flock, or the flock of one of his servants. Those he feeds upon believe lies and absurdities, follow fools and charlatans, and become gristle for the mills of his machinations."

"Hastur eats... consciousness?" Bobby asked.

"Yes," the shepherd said. The wind kept blowing, and the shepherd spoke softly. Some of his words were difficult to make out amidst the whistling. "He needs the minds to accomplish his... purpose...." Bobby thought that, after "purpose," the shepherd might have said "Bobby." The whistling, getting the better of him.

"What happened to your flock?" Sheldon asked. "What *was* your flock?"

The questions were challenges. Bobby didn't know if stirring up this guy was a good idea, but he trusted Sheldon. Guy. Was the shepherd even a guy? Bobby and Sheldon were ghosts, after all. The shepherd could have been something... else.

"Humans, demons, lesser deities... all can be consumed... all can serve his purpose...." The shepherd whispered now, whispers among whistles.

Thing One and Thing Two barked. *Woof. Woof.* Bobby felt their warnings, and their fear, in his spine.

Had the shepherd's eyes always been yellow?

"What is his purpose?" Bobby asked.

"We maintain the borders of realms and the flows across them," the shepherd said, his voice blending with the wind. His form, the white and yellow clothes, dimmed. Bobby thought he might have become slightly translucent.

"You say 'we,' meaning Hastur and who else?" Sheldon asked.

Sheldon was thinking what Bobby was thinking. *I am a man with two masters.* One of those masters was Hastur, and at some point when speaking of Hastur, the shepherd had started speaking for Hastur. Hastur might not have been welcome, but he had come.

"Who are your masters, Sheldon?" the shepherd asked.

"What if I'm my own master?" Sheldon said. Bobby didn't think the question was entirely sincere.

The shepherd laughed gently. "You won't last long."

Bobby said, "Hastur, we—"

The shepherd's eyes flooded black, and he roared, swinging his crook an inch away from striking Bobby and Sheldon. "I AM NOT!" His voice shook, and his body cramped. "We stand on the gathering ground! The challenger comes, and we organize! We will march, the Army of Ghosts! We will punish Hastur and—"

The whistling became deafening, and the slight translucence Bobby had noticed became more pronounced. The shepherd faded as he wrestled with his own body, which rebelled as muscles seemed to extend and contract unbidden. His presence thinned to nothing.

Black stars hummed.

Thing One and Thing Two whined. Bobby and Sheldon stepped back to comfort them, then stood quiet for a long while, staring at the spot where the shepherd had been.

Wind whistled through the grass, but the boys said nothing until, at last, Sheldon broke the tension: "Wow."

"Yeah," Bobby said.

"That was... dramatic," Sheldon said.

"Uh-huh," Bobby said. "I think he was a messenger. Did we get the message?"

"I sure hope so. Should we keep going?" Sheldon asked.

"Sure," Bobby said. Side by side, they continued. Thing One and Thing Two stayed very close. Bobby didn't mind.

Janet

"You're not bleeding," Heather said.

Finally, Heather was figuring out that Max was a problem that needed to take priority. "What *are* you?" Janet asked. She wished she had clothes on. Confronting someone naked sapped confidence. Granted, he was naked, too. But maybe he wasn't even a "he."

Max reached for Heather. She stepped away, toward Janet. Good.

"We just got attacked by the goddamned grass turning into... needles... and you're worried about how thick my skin is?" Max said. He was almost convincing.

"Okay," Heather said. "We can put it that way. Thorns and the goddamned grass attacked us of their own volition, and you seem to have come away from the attacks without a scratch, whereas Janet and I are damn near about to suffer deaths from a thousand cuts."

Janet looked at her pile of clothes. Getting dressed would mean bleeding all over her underwear, shorts, and shirt. Shoes and socks, too, but one of her socks already had blood on it. But where was her head? "You brought us here!" she shouted, not wanting to leave Heather alone on offense. "You knew what kind of place this was!"

"I didn't!" Max said, raising his hands defensively.

"WHAT ARE YOU?" Janet demanded.

"I DON'T KNOW!" Max cried, his posture melting, his face near tears. "I think...."

Heather was calmer, more forgiving. "What don't you know, Max Gracey? What do you think you are?"

"I think I might be... dead," Max said. "I think I might be a ghost. I... woke up... and I had this knowledge, this *purpose*... to lead you... into The Middle Reaches. It comes to me, a little at a time. I'm shepherding you through, maybe all the way... all the way to... Carcosa? Does 'Carcosa' mean anything to you?"

Janet found the answer shocking, but at the same time, she couldn't think of any answer that wouldn't have been shocking other than "some random teenage boy," and that was an answer she wouldn't have accepted. Dead? A ghost? A shepherd-ghost? Car-what-a?

Psycho-killers who vanish into thin air? Living vines and malicious grass?

From nearby came the sound of laughter, masculine, half-muffled. Then again, so many noises, the rustling, the birds, the bugs—

Looking in the direction Janet thought the sound had come from, Heather said, "Did you hear—

And from that direction came a very loud, "NOW!"

Steven

Bobby's pretty babysitter and the other naked girl were ganging up on Max, who was also naked and looked like he was in good shape, maybe a good fighter, about him not bleeding like he was supposed to, which seemed a little weird until Gordon whispered in Steven's ear that the girls were finally figuring out that Max was already dead, and then Steven understood well enough.

Gordon laughed after Max admitted to being dead, and the babysitter said, "Did you hear—"

But Gordon didn't let her finish. He gave the signal: "NOW!"

Gordon had said, "run at them," which to Steven meant no need to be sneaky at all, so Steven let out a barbaric yell as he burst from the bushes, raised the hatchet in the air, and charged at the naked and unwary trio. Gordon charged beside him, yelling as well, razor at ready. Steven imagined how they looked, a zooming nightmare, and felt proud.

Max and the two naked girls didn't even see them until they were almost there, and then, their minds too addled by Max's ghost stuff, they didn't comprehend. Max and the babysitter reversed toward the needle-grass, and the white girl stood frozen.

Gordon got to the white girl and tackled her. On top of her, he pinned her with two knees and one hand, the other hand free to wield the razor. She screamed.

Steven stopped running in a position between Max and the babysitter, and he swung the hatchet at them both. Max backed up further, so Steven went toward the babysitter, but he couldn't help watching Gordon, who striped the white girl, the white-and-red girl, with the razor. So many thin lines spilling over with red, and Gordon on top of the girl, riding delight as he cut.

Max said something. It might have been "Heather." It might have been "Faster."

Heather! That was the babysitter's name!

He wanted the hatchet to hit Heather right between the tits.

EPISODE 24: THE OLD KING AND THE NEW

Heather

The mad imp of a twelve-year-old boy got closer and closer with his hatchet already making chopping motions in the air. Not far away Max was saying, no, *chanting* her name, "Heather, Heather, Heather," like standing there naked she was supposed to do something for him, and he wasn't going to help her, or

Oh my God what's happening to Janet?

She could see, from the corner of her eye, Gordon on top of the only girl Heather had ever kissed, Janet splayed and pinned, with lines on her face, her breasts, her narrow hips, her legs that were long even without the emphasis added by the short shorts she always wore, bleeding lines. Gordon cut.

And cut. What had Heather just been saying about death by a thousand cuts? Gordon didn't want Janet to die. Not quickly. He was having fun. Getting off. Ironically, Heather was as close as she was ever likely to get to seeing what the last hours of Annie and Chris Ledbetter had been like, to watching them—

Die. They were going to die here. Steven stared at her tits. He didn't seem interested. He seemed like he was aiming.

They were going to die here, and Max wasn't saying "Heather, Heather, Heather." It was "Haster, Haster, Haster." Except the -ter sounded more like -toor. Has-toor.

Hastur.

Steven swung the hatchet at her chest. She caught his wrist in both hands, freezing his downward arc in mid-air. He pushed. She pushed back, grunting.

Max said, "Hastur."

"A little help, maybe?" Heather glanced at Max before refocusing all effort on keeping the hatchet away. Max was taller than she remembered. She was fighting for her life, and she was thinking about the height of the boy she'd just fucked.

His eyes were also yellow.

"Stop," he said.

The tense push-and-push-back between Heather and Steven released. Steven's resistance gave way, and Heather shoved him to the ground. Not wasting a moment, she spun toward Janet.

Gordon's body still pinned her, but he wasn't moving. Janet screamed. She'd been screaming the whole time, but Heather had stopped noticing.

Heather rammed Gordon, who rolled to the ground beside Janet, bloody razor still in his hand. Heather should have pursued the advantage with him—he could have struck back— he *should* have struck back—but she could only stare at Janet. Every part of her bled. Her screaming tapered to cries and moans.

"Go," Max said. His voice sounded mixed, like more than one person talking, almost like a chord. "Back where you came from."

Simultaneously, Gordon and Steven lifted themselves from the ground. "This can't be happening," Gordon said. "Not again."

Heather watched agape as the Marks boys retreated to the bushes, slipped into the trees, and were gone. Janet's noises brought her back. "Janet, I...," she said. "I don't know what to do."

Max's eyes had returned to their normal brown, and he crouched near Janet's feet. "I'll get most of her weight by lifting at the knees, but you lift at the shoulders and keep her head up."

Heather looked at him, dumbfounded. Already being dead didn't mean he wasn't obligated to make sense.

"I need you to help me carry her into the creek," he said. He stood and gathered their clothing. "We can use shirts and underwear to try to bind the places that are cut deep, but then, it's up to the creek."

"What... the fuck... are you talking about?" Heather said, standing and taking her shorts from Max's collection. She put them on while she studied the bleeding mess of Janet, who cried and quivered. How could they tell which cuts were the deep ones?

"Look for the places that are bloodiest, I guess," Max said as if he were reading her thoughts. He zipped up his pants. "Use the rest of this stuff to tie—"

"P-please," Janet said, fighting for control. "C-clothes."

Moving made cuts spread wider and must have hurt like hell, but Janet helped them get her shorts on. Janet also insisted on her bra even though the cuts on her breasts would bleed right through. Heather didn't care about her bra and used hers along with the other clothes to help Max tie up the places that seemed to be hemorrhaging the most.

"Now you want to put her in *the creek*? Forget death by a thousand cuts. Try death by a million infections," Heather said.

"I know... okay? It'll help," Max, who didn't bleed, said with a need to be believed.

Heather did believe him. She did because she knew, too. When they'd crossed the creek, she'd felt the water in the places where the thorns had gashed her wrists, and it had soothed her.

Max was right. It would help Janet, too.

Janet was becoming incoherent. She babbled, like the creek.

They carried her down to where the cleansing current flowed toward a pinker and pinker sky.

Gordon

They did not "go back where they came from." Something —something Gordon very much hated and wanted to meet alone, odds evened—had given that miserable... wannabe... Max Gracey the ability to whisk them away, AGAIN, from their task involving the babysitter and the girl Gordon had decorated, but the ability had not gone as far as setting Gordon and Steven's destination.

He was beginning to feel like the fucking coyote chasing the fucking roadrunner, but at least they hadn't come from here.

In fact, they'd never been here before.

"Where are we?" Steven asked. A fair question, but annoying because he didn't know the answer.

You are part of the timeless clockwork.

That voice in his head, like Adam's and like nobody's. Telling riddles. Behind them, dead land covered in dead grass stretched out for what looked like forever, and ahead of them, more deadness, but with stones, gravestones, crumbling, leaning this way and that, a massive, forgotten cemetery. No clockwork!

Why not be honest? "Don't know," Gordon said. "Graveyard, I guess." He headed out among the neglected stones. Steven followed.

What he really couldn't explain was the sky. Streaks of color moved through it like cars on scribbled expressways,

111

avoiding the three moons that looked bejeweled like tchotchkes at a mall kiosk. Black stars still hung in the sky like they did in the Inner Layers of The Middle Reaches. They hung even lower. The noises weren't like The Middle Reaches. Gordon heard a bass *hum* from above.

Maybe...

You are not in The Middle Reaches.

So maybe this is...

Beyond the Gate. Carcosa.

Carcosa?

Carcosa, Carcosa, Carcosa.

"A graveyard in... Carcosa," Gordon said.

Steven seemed on the verge of response when he fell silent, straining to hear other voices, *the same* voices they'd heard earlier.

"That was... dramatic," the older boy said.

"Uh-huh," the younger boy—he had to be Bobby Lightfoot —said. "I think he was a messenger. Did we get the message?"

Steven said, "That's—"

"Shhh," Gordon said. He continued in a whisper: "They'll run if we surprise them. We need to meet them where they won't run."

Steven looked confused, but he nodded. The whistling wind made sounds hard to pinpoint, but Gordon thought he could tell where Bobby was. Funny to go from being so close to one of your prey, to one purpose, and then to show up so close to another. Steven had to know Gordon's promise was bullshit. He had his razor. His razor wanted more feeding.

"Should we keep going?" the older boy asked.

"Sure," Bobby said.

"Let's tail them but keep our distance," Gordon said.

Steven nodded. They moved until they could see the boys —Bobby and the one who had gone with him through the Gate —and then stayed back, straying from what looked more and more like a path so they could use some of the larger stones and the increasingly hilly landscape for cover. Predator and prey. Predator and prey. Gordon might have been like Adam in the old days. A hunter, unfettered.

He wondered if he could use the razor to cut someone's head all the way off.

Bobby and his friend followed the path as the abandoned graveyard gave way to purer desolation, sloped dirt spotted with nothing but unmarked stones and long, dead grass that whistled when the wind blew. The whistling made Steven's shoulders crowd his ears, but Gordon didn't mind it. The hum from the stars vibrated his bones. The whistle from the grass tickled his skin.

The path forked at the foot of one hill, then another. Each time, Bobby and the older boy took the path that seemed to lead most directly toward the white wall high in the distance. The wall looked like the walls that protected towns in the Dark Ages, except it was smooth. The closer they got, the surer Gordon felt that he saw things crawling up and down the rounded wall.

The path forked more often, and it curved, zigged, and zagged, and finally it brought Bobby and his friend to a stony dead end. Gordon picked up his pace. Steven followed. The prey turned and saw them coming. Gordon savored the terror in Bobby's eyes.

"Hello again," Gordon said, brandishing the razor. On all sides of the prey, the hills were steep. They could climb out, but not fast enough to escape.

"Gordon, no!" Steven yelled.

Gordon wouldn't play with the boys like he'd played with

the babysitter's friend. He wouldn't take that chance. He would go straight for their throats. He was ready to slash—

—but a hand caught his arm. No, *no, NO!*

He yanked his arm from the intruding grip and spun, ready to kill whatever motherfucker had

ADAM! ADAM FUCKING MORTIMER!

Maybe this time, it was okay. The bulky man in the bright red shirt leaned down and plucked the straight razor from Gordon's hand. Goddamn it. But maybe this time, it was okay.

Bobby

Blood-freezing terror, the whistling wind and humming stars amplified, Gordon Marks stood in front of him like he had after he'd tied Bobby to the tree, and Bobby felt the shovel's blade break his arm, and it hit him again, breaking his ribs, and when it hit his thigh, the bone didn't break, but it hurt, and the world spun around him, and he was naked and fat and ugly and going to die here.

"Hello again," Gordon said. He had a razor like Bobby's dad used. Sharp. Dad said it could cut skin like butter.

"Gordon, no!" Steven! Steven was with his brother! But Steven *hated* his brother! *Why...*

Behind Gordon, another form, bigger than all of them, an adult, a man in a red shirt. Bobby understood instantly who the man was, which explained why Sheldon had been compelled to tell him the story. He was THE man in the red shirt, avatar of the God of the Citadel.

The Citadel, through which they had to pass to enter the Walled City.

Which was scarier, the boy who'd killed him or the avatar of an evil god?

What's more terrifying, hope or despair?

Thing One and Thing Two growled, baring rows and rows of teeth. Bobby smiled.

As Gordon brought his razor down toward Bobby in an arc, Sheldon pushed Bobby back, shielding him, and Red Shirt surprised them all: he caught Gordon's arm, and as Gordon turned around, he took away the razor.

"Adam!" Gordon sounded awed. "I knew I'd find you! I knew you were part of... all of this."

"You've gone a bit rogue, sport," Red Shirt said. Adam? Was his name Adam? "School's back in session."

Thing One barked. Thing Two kept growling.

Gordon looked behind him and then met Adam's coddling expression. "I was only going to kill—

"Oh, I know," Adam said, "and I know you've killed him before, so it feels right, but this time, it isn't."

"You're Adam Mortimer," Steven said.

"And you must be Steven." Adam offered a handshake. Steven, trembling, accepted it. Adam turned to Sheldon, then Bobby. "You are... Sheldon Vere, and you are the famous Bobby Lightfoot. A pleasure to make your acquaintances."

"You're a hell of a lot more than Adam Mortimer," Sheldon said.

Thing One unleashed a flurry of barks, *woof-woof-woof-woof-woof-woof-woof*.

"Quiet, now," Adam said. "Be polite."

With fiercer explosion of noise, Thing One lunged past Gordon and soared toward Adam. Gordon and Steven stumbled back from the beast in fear and surprise, but Adam remained stolid until he caught the creature in his arms, somehow paralyzing its snapping jaw and raking claws. Adam tossed

Thing One into the stony barrier at the end of the path, where it hit and fell to the ground with a yelp.

"Tha!" Bobby yelled, not able to get out "Thing One." Keeping an eye on the others, he checked on the fallen uber-dog.

"There's a party at my place," Adam said. "There's always a party at my place. I hope you'll all attend."

Bobby didn't see any blood in Thing One's fur. All six legs looked fine. It seemed more stunned than hurt.

"To address your claim, Sheldon, I'm not more than Adam Mortimer. Adam Mortimer is simply more than most would reckon. King. God. And now your personal tour guide, here to lead you to my humble home. Won't you come?"

Janet

She had more hurt than skin, and sights and sounds, jumbled together, a flood in her ears, a strobe in her eyes, all flagellated by pain, they hopped. Someone moved her, and the hops got bigger. She was afraid of someone moving her because it could have been the monster from the bushes with the flat knife *razor* yes *razor*—

No. Heather and Max carried her. Why were they carrying her? Shouldn't they wait for the ambulance?

No. There wouldn't be an ambulance because they were... in a bad place.

She wanted to lose consciousness. Why couldn't she lose consciousness?

They carried her to the water, got into the water with her. The water. The creek! Not the creek! But then... all the holes on her back... all the slashes on the front of her that dipped below the surface... felt the water seeping inside, where every nerve screamed. The screaming got quieter. Numbness. The tide seeping in brought numbness.

Her thoughts sorted themselves.

On her back, she partly floated, and was partly carried, over the water. On her right, Heather held her arm and guided her. Max held the other arm. They were both naked from the waist up. Above her, the pink sky had a streak of red.

The bad place. The Middle Reaches.

Gordon Marks had almost killed her.

She would never be beautiful.

"I don't know what happened," Max was saying. "Not exactly, anyway."

"You kept saying 'Hastur,'" Heather said. "And your eyes...."

"What about my eyes?"

Heather's response was subdued: "They were... yellow."

"That's weird," Max said.

Janet pulled air into her lungs, and her chest hurt as it expanded. With enough breath, though, she could say, "Heather."

Heather said, "I got the feeling it was a name. Who is Hastur?" Heather didn't hear her?

"He is... I...." Max fumbled. "You know how I was... *sent*... to you? He's the one who sent me. I... serve... him. Everyone in The Middle Reaches serves someone."

"Even me?" Heather asked.

"I don't know," Max said.

"Heather," Janet repeated, louder.

Heather said, "So, with Gordon and Steven, Hastur..."

"Hastur doesn't want them to stop you. And I'm pretty sure he's older and more powerful than the one *they* serve," Max said.

Janet managed to turn her head more toward Heather while keeping her mouth and nose out of the water. Powerful forces looking after her. Of course. Who better?

Certainly not Janet.

"And Hastur is related to that place you mentioned," Heather said. "Carcosa."

"Yes. I will take you to him. Unless I fail." Max looked down at her, but Janet wouldn't turn her head back toward him to meet his gaze. "No one has complete control of The Middle Reaches. Gordon and Steven could try again. Or worse."

Chivalrous Max would escort the anointed Lady Heather to her appointment with the Great Hastur. Each of them had a role, a purpose. And where did that leave her? She was...

Expendable. Most Likely To Die.

"Heather!" Janet said.

Heather looked down at her. "Max, I think she's lucid. Janet, is there something we can do?" "We." Heather and Max were a "we." Janet was worse than a third wheel. She was baggage. Broken, bleeding baggage.

And although she wanted to say so much to Heather, she knew she was talking to the wrong person. She clenched her jaw and turned her head. "Max," she said.

"I'm here for you," he said, looking down at her with a comforting, small smile. He was cute and nice and kind of loathsome.

Water surrounded her, but Janet's throat felt dry. "Where," she said, and she stopped to swallow. "Where do I fit? You, Heather, Hastur, Carcosa. What about me?"

She knew what his answer would be. It was his answer to most questions: "I don't know."

Sheldon

The "famous" Bobby Lightfoot walked between Thing One and Thing Two, a hand almost always stroking Thing One's fur. Sheldon walked on Thing One's other side. The animal (loosely construed) didn't have the slightest limp. Bobby's concern for it was irritating. He hadn't even acknowledged what Sheldon... anyways. "You know, hurting one of those, um, uber-dogs is difficult, killing one next to impossible."

What Sheldon said was true, but on the other hand, if anyone could kill one of those creatures, a god's avatar would be a very good candidate.

"Okay," Bobby said.

Adam and Gordon led their newly expanded group, side by side at the front, making choices when the path offered them. Bobby, Sheldon, and the two Things took the rear, and Steven floated in the middle, alone. Sheldon expected Bobby to approach Gordon's little brother. He knew Bobby's relationship with Steven had been... special. At the moment, Steven didn't seem related to anyone.

Sheldon thought of Nick.

"We're dead," Bobby said, still stroking Thing One, "so I guess being scared of Gordon and Adam is stupid."

Sheldon looked down at his bare feet. His toes were cold. The Old City grew colder and colder the closer they got to the New City's towering white wall. Sheldon didn't know about Gordon, but he knew being scared of Adam was *not* stupid. He wouldn't say that, though. Instead, he said, "Death has its privileges."

"Excuse me," Bobby said. He sped up, passed Steven without a word, and nudged in between Gordon and Adam, repeating, "Excuse me."

119

Gordon looked down at him. Sheldon had to imagine the look of murder on his face.

"Give the young man some room, sport," Adam said. Sheldon felt glad the whistles and *hum* were soft enough for him to hear what Adam said, but he didn't want to miss anything. As Thing One and Thing Two tightened their distance from Bobby, flanking Steven, Sheldon stayed close behind them.

Steven, obviously disturbed by uber-dog proximity, drifted back to Sheldon's side.

"I'm not afraid of you," Bobby said to Adam.

Sheldon couldn't see Adam's face. He and Steven looked at each other.

"I don't need your fear, kiddo. I need you," Adam said. Sheldon felt a wave of resentment.

"Why me?" *Why do doors keep opening for me?*

"Let me tell you a story," Adam said.

"Long ago, before evolved monkeys in your realm figured out fire, the sky in Carcosa had one color, yellow, and the land, lake, and inhabitants flourished in their ways. Carcosa had one King, the King in Yellow, of whom you've heard... later called God of the Palace and Hastur. He ruled in a grand city located where we now walk. The King had appetites—his Court was madness—but he did not over-indulge.

"The King rarely reached into other realms, but curiosity and an indelible yearning for more did propel him to reach, and reaching captured the attention of others. First, one came powerful enough to seek domain in the lake, Lake Hali, and the King granted it. Another came, however, who would not be content with some... parcel... of the beautiful Kingdom. He wanted to become the new King.

"The resulting war broke the sky and destroyed the legendary city of Carcosa, but the old King's victory was decisive.

The old King did not, and I might say could not, kill or banish the pretender, so instead he invited him to a meeting in the new Palace at the heart of the new Carcosa.

"At the meeting was a three-sided table. Three attended. The old King led, proposing that all three become Kings. The old King would be High King in the Palace, the ruler of Lake Hali would maintain sovereignty there, and the pretender would have a castle, a Citadel, built into the new Carcosa's wall, the only entrance and exit for the Walled City.

"An uneasy peace that let them—and you know I mean us—feed all our appetites began. We are often at odds, seldom in unison, but we have never come again to open conflict. Our reaches have multiplied and spread so widely that another war would be catastrophic across many realms."

"But something changed," Bobby said. "What?"

"You, kiddo," Adam said. "You. You brought *him*."

"Who...?"

Sheldon knew the answer before Adam continued.

"The one you *are* afraid of," Adam said. "You call him—"

Bobby and Adam's voices blended, quivering tenor and sonorous bass: "The Man in the Grinning Mask."

"He wants Carcosa, but he'll use it to access other realms," Adam said. "His appetite for chaos is absolute. We can have no peace. Hastur and Avin, which is to say Hastur and I, are more closely allied than we have ever been in our desire to be rid of him, of the destruction he represents. Bobby, your dreams let him out. You may hold the key to stopping him."

Huh. So, Bobby unleashed a force that could destroy the universe. Figures. *A special kind of guy*.

EPISODE 25: CITADEL OF GLASS

Heather

She'd fucked a dead guy.

She found many aspects of her situation disturbing and difficult to fathom, including the subpoint that the dead guy she'd fucked served a god or entity of a sort that Heather would have said yesterday could not exist, but the broader condition of her intimacy with Max's deadness struck her as most profound.

Heather and Max the Dead Boy helped Heather's friend Janet, who'd been sliced to ribbons quite recently by a young psychopath who'd had the kindness to leave when Max the Dead Boy had given the order, float on a creek with narcotic properties. It was a creek along which, and within which, one had to be vigilant for monsters.

Such as the bulky, furry, four-appendaged thing that she supposed most resembled a small bear, except its paws were more like talons, and its face was mostly a flat hole from which a very long, prehensile tongue projected, taking whole birds as prey as it leapt—far too high—toward the red-and-purple-streaked sky.

Max must have seen the growing tension in her face as they neared the place where the bulky creature ambled on the shore. "Don't worry," he said. "It won't bother us as long as we stay in the water and keep moving."

"Is that one of the things you know?" Heather asked. "The way you, you know, know things?"

"Sure," he said. He was not good at being comforting. But then again, he was dead. Perhaps, if she were dead, she wouldn't invest a lot of mental energy in being comforting, either.

If she were Janet, would she wish she were dead? Coming up with comforting things to say to her childhood friend wasn't exactly easy. The creek had washed away a lot of the blood, leaving a reddish sheen on much of Janet's skin, but so much of Janet was ripped and clotting. Gordon had done such extensive damage. Heather had seen him cut her. The image in her mind inspired nausea. It had been—

Hypnotic.

At her side, floating between her and a dead kid, Janet was a sketch drawn with scabs.

A sketch by someone legendary. People would write books about Gordon Marks. People like Janet.

Though maybe not Janet.

Max was the Dead Boy who Served Some Deity. Janet was the Scab Sketch. Heather inhaled through her nose and felt a smile on her cheeks. Both of her companions' statuses added to their allure. Perhaps Janet's especially. Before she had been... fine, but plain. Now she was extraordinary. Her skin would tell the story of her encounter with Gordon Marks for the rest of her life, however long that might be.

Something underwater brushed by her bare calf. She wouldn't feel, look, or stop. She would follow the creek, keeping the Scab Sketch afloat, gazing, from time to time, with contentment at Max the Shirtless Dead Boy with a Nice Tan.

"Do I have to be alive?" Heather asked.

"What?" Max asked, evidently startled by how she had broken a long silence.

"You're taking me to your leader," Heather said, hoping he wouldn't mind the joke. He didn't seem to notice. "To Hastur, I mean. When I get there, do I have to be alive?"

"Yes! You must live!" He acted as if she'd suggested cutting her own throat. "Heather lives," he said, calming. "Heather has to live."

"It's only... ever since I ran into that... Shadow Man... I've had this... deep... fragile feeling... like I'm made of glass. Like I'm made of glass, and I'll be better off when I'm broken." Heather took a deep breath, enjoying the effect of the air on her nerves. "So why?" she asked. "Being dead hardly seems to faze you at all. Why do I have to be alive?"

A pause lingered.

"I don't know," Max said.

Sheldon

Adam and Gordon, with Bobby in between, Thing One and Thing Two close behind, and Sheldon by Steven in the rear, followed a curving path over the crest of a hill, and then, the three moons above it, its four luminous, colored spires stabbing into the already color-addled sky, the Glass Citadel stood in plain sight.

The spires' conical rooves, orange, green, blue, and yellow, were easiest to see, but the remainder of the Citadel wreaked havoc on the eyes. Sheldon saw opulent rooms with fantastic people moving along corridors and stairways, but he also saw erasing glare, refractions of blinding light, rainbows beaming through a structure superficially like the white wall at its sides, curving barrier and high battlements.

Unlike the high wall of bone, however, the Glass Citadel had many small windows with narrow Gothic arches—they looked defensive—and at its center, an immense door, also a

Gothic arch, was covered in symbols of different sizes, some of which Sheldon could see even from this distance. They looked similar to the writing from Lost Carcosa.

"The towers on your castle," Bobby said. "The colors mean something, don't they?"

"Yes," Adam said.

"Will you tell me what they mean?"

"If you like," Adam said. "Pain is... elemental, and I have long been interested in the connections between pain and elemental forces, earth, air, fire, and water. I have also had an interest in varieties of pain, which some have said can be reduced to five categories, hot, cold, blunt, piercing, and shocking. When I oversaw the construction of the Citadel, I came to a four-spire compromise, orange for fire and heat, blue for water and cold, yellow for air, electricity, and more advanced technology, and green for wood, metal, and basic tools and machines. Some categorization is a bit arbitrary, I admit, but over the millennia our scheme has held up remarkably well for the areas we've wished to explore. We've chronicled agonies the count of which is now a matter of debate, invented tortures even the most adventurous of earthly imaginations would find unimaginable. The system works for us because we work for it."

"People?" Bobby said. "You torture people?"

Sheldon stifled a laugh.

"Much of the time," Adam said, not at all impatient with the question.

"Does Ellie know about all of this?" Gordon asked.

Who was Ellie?

Adam bent down to Bobby. "Ellie, my wife. Adam's wife. She, Gordon, and I did some work together." Adam straightened. They were walking downhill, picking up speed, and the immense symbol-covered door loomed closer and closer. "If she knows, I didn't tell her. We parted shortly after we entered The Middle Reaches. I suspect she... but that's not important."

The Middle Reaches. The term sounded strange coming out of Adam's mouth because, at least to his recollection, Sheldon had invented it. Sheldon didn't invent the weirdness between the two Acton Ways—that was there already—but he had named the place and built up the lore around it, bringing in Ambrose Bierce and Robert W. Chambers. God of the Palace, God of the Lake, God of the Citadel—those were Sheldon's flourishes.

Now they were real, and they had details Sheldon had never imagined, like the God of the Citadel being named Avin and Avin having an avatar named Adam, shit Sheldon hadn't bothered to dream up. Shit that had evolved on its own, or had always been real but had never manifested through Sheldon's story-spinning. Shit like—

The Man in the Grinning Mask. Bobby had made him up, or at least dreamed him, and he turned out to be real like Sheldon's imaginings turned out to be real, but for some reason, Bobby turned out to be the Chosen One and Sheldon turned out to be—

Walking in the back with Steven.

Steven

Sunset with no sun. Carcosa got dimmer, all at once, everywhere, and the jeweled moons lost their brilliance, and the sky's moving streaks faded through grey toward what seemed like an inevitable black that would hide the humming stars.

"Darkfall," Adam said. The wind whistling through dead grass almost masked his voice.

The whiteness of the New City's wall resisted the fade, shining against the dark, but it wasn't a white of hope, or cleanness, or purity. Steven felt but didn't think of it as the marble pallor lingering in the aspect of the dead whose all-pervading quality appeared more strangely hideous than the ugliest abortion. Bobby talked about symbols. Whatever people tried to make white symbolize, this white tied the hue with death.

The death Steven and Gordon brought to others.

The death Bobby had experienced.

The death that seemed like part of Adam's voice.

"Night? I thought it was nighttime already," Bobby said to Adam. Bobby walked with Adam and Gordon. He paid no attention to Steven. Steven didn't exist.

The Glass Citadel sparkled within the wall, lit, too, as if by a source of its own, gilded picture frames on transparent walls, luxurious furniture, glamorous people. On the Citadel's front, climbing around the door and windows on the sheer surface, pale grey creatures cast shadows with their wings and horns. One of them leapt from the wall and twisted through the air around the blue spire.

"We're close, but Darkfall is usually brief," Adam said, "and we should stop. I can build a fire from the grass. Rest might be helpful anyway."

Rest? Like *sleep*? Steven couldn't remember the last time he'd slept.

"You won't sleep," Adam said. "Some might collapse from exhaustion, and sometimes, we dream, but here, nobody sleeps."

"Why stop?" Sheldon said. "Something scary in the dark? Even for you?"

Adam looked back over his shoulder at Sheldon. His gaze passed over Steven before he again faced forward. "We have enemies in the dark. In the dark, the wind has hands. It has wings."

Steven looked back toward the Glass Citadel, at the

creature flying circles around the blue spire. It was big. He hadn't figured out a true sense of the Citadel's proportions yet, but he knew the creature was big. Big horns, broad wings, and... reptilian... features.

Minutes later, they sat around a fire near stones beside the path. Sheldon, Bobby, Adam, and Gordon made an arc. Thing One and Thing Two lay behind Bobby, nervously shifting positions every few seconds. Steven sat opposite the arc, further from the fire, on his own.

The whistling wind would require them almost to shout at one another. Except for the firelight that made a dome around them, and the wall and Citadel not too far away, darkness was total. Had they kept walking, they wouldn't have been able to see their feet on the path.

Sheldon said something. Adam responded. Gordon said something. Bobby responded. Steven couldn't hear. Drifting in null space, he hugged his knees and buried his face between them.

Someone tapped his shoulder. "Mind if I sit with you?"

Steven looked up. Bobby was asking permission. "Sure," Steven said. The boys sat together, looking at the fire. Steven felt cold.

"So," Bobby said. "You and Gordon are a team now. The Marks brothers."

"Sort of," Steven said. "A lot happened after you... disappeared." He shivered. "You and Adam seem to be teaming up." Adam was talking to Sheldon. Steven didn't trust Sheldon, either.

The wind whistled. It ruffled his hair and bit through his summer clothes. It passed behind him like a figure in fans of long fabric.

"Not teaming up," Bobby said. "It's practical. He's the power."

"We saw him," Steven said. He'd walked under the bright blue sky to the other Acton Way, where the closest house's back deck angled toward the dead end. He'd climbed up the stairs, terrified, and gone into the house. "When we were trying to find out what happened to you, we saw him."

"'We' means..."

"Me and Chris. We went into his house because we knew Gordon had been going there. He chased us. Wearing a bright red shirt he chased us, and he was... you're right, powerful. The red shirt. We imagined he could have been... it seemed stupid...." Steven looked through the fire at Adam, in a different shirt of the same color, talking to Sheldon. Gordon listened intently.

"This place has a way of making anything you could imagine seem not so stupid," Bobby said.

"We imagined Adam *was* The Man in the Grinning Mask," Steven said. Through the flames, he made brief eye contact with Adam before the man turned his head back toward Sheldon. Had Adam heard? Steven couldn't make out a word from Adam's side of the fire, but Adam, and power—

"That's not a stupid idea at all," Bobby said. The wind almost drowned his words. Steven shivered and clenched his jaw to keep his teeth from chattering. Again, he felt a sensation like a swoosh of long fabric, or the slow flapping of a giant wing, from movement behind him.

Steven tried to concentrate. "What if it's all a trick? What if Adam is The Man in the Grinning Mask?"

Someone tapped Steven's shoulder. The tap was like Bobby's from moments before, but no one was there, and its pressure left behind a spot like ice.

"We fight," Bobby said. "We might have to fight him anyway, I don't know. But if and when we have to, we fight like we always did in Dimension X."

Steven rubbed his icy shoulder and looked behind him

into pitch black. *We have enemies in the dark.* "Dimension X was make-believe. We never really fought anybody. This is real."

Bobby cast his eyes toward the Glass Citadel. Steven knew what he meant before he asked, "Are you sure?"

Steven allowed a small laugh before he said, "I guess I—"

Cold hands wrapped around his neck and pulled. He slid over the ground, away from the fire until he couldn't see anything. Cold spread like water splashing from hands choking him and pouring over the rest of his body. He couldn't scream. He couldn't see. Help could have been close, or it could have been a million miles away. He was frozen, breathless, and unable to struggle.

Bobby, please! Gordon, please! SOMEBODY! EVERYBODY! DON'T LEAVE ME!

Seconds might have been minutes that might have been hours that might have been—

Another hand wrapped around his ankle and pulled. He was a rope tugged back and forth by warring forces, skin stretching between deep cold and an iota of the fire's warmth.

"GOT YOU!" a man's voice roared.

Steven soared higher, vision returned, and the fire passed beneath him. His body crashed into another, and arms held him. Sobs wanted to escape. Arms held him. "I've got you."

Steven looked to see who held him.

"I've got you," Adam repeated. "You're one of mine. Nobody's going to take you." His flat voice was factual, not reassuring.

Nevertheless, Steven felt warm.

Janet

The air, too. Like the water, the air was a drug, a cross

between Oxy and MDMA, maybe, with a hint of speed, because she accepted that, no matter the pain, the horror, *the wish not to be*, she would stay conscious, alert, even interested in her surroundings, in Heather topless, in the things that slithered and creeped.

Her cuts had turned to scabs, which meant she was healing with tremendous speed, which she understood to be supernatural, and she didn't know how much credit to give the creek and how much credit to give the touch of Max the Friendly and Sexually Adventurous Ghost. She felt like if she had more information, she might be able to wrap her mind around how this supernatural stuff worked.

Anything was possible. That was clear enough.

Heather probably thought she was in a state of silent agony, but really, Janet was in an intellectual frame of mind, disinclined to speak her analytical thoughts about her situation. She understood that, if she survived, she'd need to subscribe to a reality involving her being attacked in the neighborhood rather than in a supernatural realm. All mentions of the supernatural would be scrubbed from her narrative.

In short, she'd need to omit the most compelling parts. Her experiences had ramifications for how most people perceived the universe. They turned lowbrow fiction into high-consequences fact. If people believed her, she'd change the world. If people wouldn't assume she was crazy, she'd be the most important journalist who ever lived.

As she floated through a whirlpool littered with human flesh and bone, she had to admit to herself that her experiences were absolutely batshit crazy.

Max halted their progress not long after a mist rose over the creek and surrounding area. "We have to get out of the water," he said.

Heather scoffed. "You said we have to stay IN the water!"

"There are creatures in the creek ahead we can't pass by without getting hurt," Max said. "Category of things I know."

"There are things...." Heather looked around, flustered. "What about those caterpillar things?"

"Further back," Max said. "Come on," he said. "We have to."

"What about Janet?"

I think I can walk. Say it aloud! "I think I can... I think I'll be... okay."

Heather leaned over her. "Okay if we carry you? I don't think we'll make it very far—"

"I can walk," Janet said.

Heather's befuddled expression was very cute.

The transition from lying in the water to twisting, standing upright, and operating her arms and legs—all of which broke scabs—was the most painful. Janet huffed the narcotic air and tried to concentrate on, without staring at, Heather's tits. Soon, the threesome followed the creek, which dwindled almost to a trickle. They came to a kind of mound, a lump of stone with a face of roots and vines.

"The Cavern of The Mouth," Max said.

"Nah," Heather said. "That doesn't sound ominous."

It only gets better from here, Janet thought. She felt disinclined to speak aloud.

Gordon

Why would Adam need a door this big? What giants would he have to let in or out of his castle?

The Glass Citadel. It didn't seem to *fit* Adam, or Avin, or whatever he would be going forward. Adam seemed more like brick than glass. Gordon didn't doubt the Citadel was strong, but it looked fancy, and as he approached, he saw fancy people inside, some looking like people from the courts of kings and queens in the old days and some looking like people from magazines in doctors' offices.

Fancy. Not Adam. Adam was simple. Primal.

The symbols on the door, which was stone, not glass, were fancy, too, different sizes and silver and gold. Gordon didn't know what the dots, squiggles, and lines meant, and he didn't really care.

"What does it mean?" Bobby asked.

"Did you read *The Iliad* in school?" Adam asked.

"Not in school," Bobby said.

Gordon hated English class. He wanted the goddamned doors to open.

"It is similar," Adam said. Yay. Adam hadn't given back his razor. "It is a fuller version of the story I told you, of the conflict that gave rise to the current state of Carcosa, and the Triumvirate that rules. The language is not mine—its presence was a stipulation of the High King—but I do know it gives proper due to the story of Avin's first wife, from long before Adam was an idea."

Adam told a story, and took his damned time, about the beautiful Ginosha, whose appetite for conquest and suffering rivaled Avin's during Avin's bid for rulership of all Carcosa. Hastur learned that their... not love, but bond... could be exploited.

After a day of too-easy victories, Avin found Ginosha staked to the ramparts of his own fortifications. In palpable agony, she gazed from Avin to her limbs, stretched through long torture to many times their usual length. Her torso, too, had been divided like a harp, and tortures had stretched the strings of her so that shoulders and hips were distant neighbors. Her neck was the tallest of candlesticks, her head a spinning globe. She was beautiful.

"Kind of a spaghetti woman, eh?" Adam poked Bobby. Adam didn't smile at his own joke, and neither did the little fat fuck. Gordon smiled, though.

The point of the story was that Hastur had created such beauty from Ginosha's suffering that Avin reached his first understanding that he would be able to acknowledge Hastur as supreme.

Storytime finally ended, and the giant doors opened. Adam forged ahead, but Gordon and the others walked in slowly, probably because they were all dizzy from the scope of the Main Hall. The Hall itself was undoubtedly vast, forward, left, right, and upward, but because its boundaries were glass, they were transparent and reflective, and they added illusions of volumes of additional space.

"Infinities," Bobby said. "Infinities within infinities."

Gordon felt annoyed, but he couldn't have said it better.

After talking to some fancy people, Adam returned to them. "You must do without me for a while, but explore, with care. We prepare for the Carnival of Meat, and I must attend to our special guest."

"Guest?" Sheldon asked.

"He has no name, but you shouldn't be surprised to meet him," Adam said. "Bobby dubbed him The Man in the Grinning Mask."

Max

He had no control, but he could see, hear, and feel, and he understood what was happening. He was a conduit, a key. He would lead Heather through the Gate to Carcosa.

His hand on the wall of roots and vines made it spread apart, forming a door. The flickering lights—white, pink, red, purple—got brighter as swirling clouds came fully into view.

"You sure you're okay?" Heather asked.

"Not okay," Janet said, "but going on. Going with you."

As The Mouth appeared, rows and rows of hooked fangs, the girls caught up to Max. The Mouth aligned, and Max raised his hand toward it as it shot from the clouds toward Heather, snapping.

Heather screamed but held her ground. The Watcher wanted to stop her. Devour her. Reassign her.

As a conduit, Max made The Mouth still. The Watcher opposed Hastur's ambition, but The Mouth would obey.

Max led Heather and Janet through the Gate to Carcosa.

EPISODE 26:
MIRROR MAZE

Bobby

"I think we might have made a mistake," Bobby said.

"I think we might have made a few mistakes," Sheldon said. He looked left and right, each way a tall mirror, an inverted U reflecting an inverted U reflecting an inverted U reflecting reflections reflecting reflections, infinities within infinities. "Where to begin?"

The small portions of walls visible behind the grand mirrors were not naked glass like at the front of the Citadel. Deep red velvet covered them, which Bobby would have anticipated had he known they would end up in halls of mirrors like the ones that had led him to The Middle Reaches... lifetimes ago?

No, this hall was not *like* one of those halls. It *was* one of those halls. The Man in the Grinning Mask had chased him here, dragging his sword across the marble tiles. The Man in the Grinning Mask, *our special guest*. "Our" referred to Adam, or Avin, and his followers. Gordon and Steven were his followers. Even if "followers" wasn't the right word, they were somehow fundamentally *his*.

That was the mistake Bobby meant, except he said "we" made a mistake to be nice because it wasn't his mistake but Sheldon's because Sheldon had been the one who suggested slipping away from Gordon and Steven in the Main Hall crowd.

Gordon and Steven were distracted by... exhibits... so losing them was easy.

Bobby didn't think of staying close to people on Team Avin to gain protection, not until he realized they'd stumbled into a hall of mirrors he'd been in before, and going back wouldn't help them, and—

They weren't alone.

Wishing for Gordon Marks to be nearby for protection. It was sick. But he had seen, in the corners of the mirrors, at the edges of his vision, the same creatures that climbed the white wall, that crept up and down the Citadel's glass façade, and that circled the high spires, flapping broad, featherless wings.

The creatures were grey, smooth, slick, like stone. They had horns on heads that looked like dinosaurs' and clawed feet that clicked on the marble tiles as they crept, lizard-like, wings tucked back, behind Bobby and Sheldon, possibly ahead of them, too—

The only word Bobby had for them was *gargoyles*. Gargoyles stalked them through the halls of mirrors. Bobby didn't know how many there were. Infinities of infinities.

Sheldon lingered in front of a mirror, gazing at their reflections. Either he wasn't glimpsing their pursuers, or he didn't care. "Sheldon," Bobby said, fighting to make his voice clear, "we've got to—"

"Why are they like that?" Sheldon asked.

Thing One and Thing Two stood close to Bobby. He had a sense of them now, nervous, baring their teeth, holding their ears back, puffing their fur. They weren't as big as the gargoyles. Sheldon said hurting an uber-dog was difficult, killing one next to impossible, but Thing One had the scar on its nose. They understood pain. They understood fear.

They understood being in the presence of something higher on the food chain.

Sheldon wasn't asking about them. Bobby searched around. He didn't see horns or wings, in the hall or in the mirrors. He still didn't think they were alone. He had a sense. Reluctantly, he joined Sheldon in gazing at the mirror. "Why are who like what?" Bobby asked.

"Don't you see?" Sheldon said, not taking his eyes from the mirror.

Frustrated, Bobby looked at their reflections. He looked like he was supposed to look, and Sheldon, taller, handsomer, fitter, looked like he was supposed to look, and—

and their positions were reversed.

Bobby gulped. He had awakened between the Acton Ways, gone to the creek, and instead of his reflection, he had seen an unknown boy who had turned out to be Sheldon, pale skin and ice blue eyes. Now he reflected Sheldon again, and Sheldon reflected him. *Why?*

Click, click, click. Long, sharp, thick claws on marble tile.

Bobby repeated, "We've got to—"

"Get moving," Sheldon finished. "I know."

They wandered further into the mirror maze.

Gordon

Hot, cold, blunt, piercing, and shocking didn't cover *tons* of possibilities for hurting people, and Adam had to know, so the whole scheme he'd laid out for his castle's neon towers was complete bullshit. Gordon had the perfect example right in front of him, one of the exhibits for the Carnival of Meat.

He couldn't tell how many exhibits were involved in the almost complete set-up process because each was a glass cage on a glass pedestal in the glass-walled Main Hall, every bit of structure translucent, so getting the big picture of how many were in the room posed the same difficulty as figuring out the size of the Main Hall, too many reflections and refractions that led to too much distortion and uncertainty.

Gordon liked it, actually—seeing echoes of objects that seemed emancipated from normal space—but to see the exhibit in front of him, he had to look through a faint image of himself, which he didn't like. He couldn't not look at it, though. Why hadn't he thought of it immediately while Adam was talking about the five types of pain—it was obvious! Hunger!

"They're so calm," Steven said. "Do you think they... do it on purpose? Or are they prisoners who... gave up?"

Two naked people—if "people" was still a fair term—a man and a woman, if—sat on opposite sides of the glass box, legs extended, backs slumped, both rocking gently with the heartbeats visible in the veins and arteries on display through paper-thin skin. The skin covered, in places not erased by sores, skeletons articulated through minimal flesh. They looked like their breaths might break them.

Gordon didn't understand how they could still be alive. Deprived of food, their bodies had eaten themselves.

He laughed. "Maybe they just couldn't find anything good to eat." He laughed again. "What I want to know... I mean, they're too weak now, but at some point they must have thought about going after each other. You know, a fight to the death, then a feast."

"Maybe they care about each other," Steven said. He gave the emaciated bodies a long look. "Or used to. Maybe it's just hard to eat somebody with other people watching."

Gordon looked at his little brother. He was growing up in good ways.

When Gordon turned back to the glass, he almost jumped. Instead of his own faint reflection between himself and the starving couple, he saw Adam's, or a younger Adam, not as muscular but still imposing. He had a familiar expression on a slightly more angular face.

Gordon looked behind him. No Adam. The reflection was his, or ought to have been. Somehow, he projected an Adam-image.

The Adam-image wasn't all there. Gaps appeared in his arms, chest, cheek, and forehead. A moment ago, Gordon's reflection had been faint but complete. Something kept this reflection from being whole.

If the reflection meant they were connected, and Gordon *knew* they were, did it mean the connection was partial? Did it mean Gordon was like Adam, but only like some of him? Only *worth* some of him? The way Adam talked to Bobby... was Gordon losing Adam a little at a time?

Stupid fucking reflection. Stupid fucking questions. "Steven?"

Gordon turned to direct Steven's attention to the Adam-image, but when the brothers looked together at the glass, the image was gone.

Heather

"After Bobby told me about him, I dreamed about him, too. Only, my dreams add a black top hat. A magician's hat. He reaches down toward his feet and pulls rabbits out of nowhere. He stuffs the rabbits in his hat, and they disappear. A magic trick, but backward. For some reason, it scares the hell out of me. *He* scares the hell out of me."

The Man in the Grinning Mask. As they walked on this somehow-suspended land bridge away from the Gate and the green emptiness, Heather didn't know whether they moved toward Bobby Lightfoot or toward the truth about what happened to him—though she had no reason to distrust Max, his death notwithstanding—but she did know they moved toward *him*.

She *knew* the way Max *knew* things. Carcosa seemed like a knowing kind of place.

And she knew *it*. Carcosa. She didn't know whether she'd been here before, but it was familiar. Looking out at Lake Hali, she felt unsurprised by the ruddy water, changing highlights with the shifting smears of color in the sky, or the deep blue crystalline shore. She knew the mists were fire and poison, and she knew that within them, life teemed... along with a singular presence, an acquaintance she would make.

But not now. Now, they would go to the Glass Citadel, which she couldn't see from the place where they walked, but she could see it in her mind, tricks of light that multiplied infinities.

A magic trick, but backward. That's how she'd described her dream of The Man in the Grinning Mask to Janet. The Man wielded his sword like a magician's wand. He shoved rabbits into his black top hat instead of pulling them out. It seemed so perverse, like shoving a baby back into the womb. Was it erasing a life by pushing it before its beginning?

"Heather, are you okay?" Janet asked.

Was *she* okay? Janet was a walking wound, and she asked if *Heather* was okay. "Yeah, I think so." *The way your broken scabs seep blood and pus turns me on.* "I just have a weird feeling."

Janet either laughed or coughed. "I think we had our last normal feelings sometime around breakfast."

Heather snickered. "You're probably right."

Max, walking ahead, stopped, so Heather and Janet stopped. A path branched to their left, into a desolate field, and another continued ahead, toward the lake and the towering white wall. Max gestured toward the field. "Most of Lost Carcosa is that way. So is the shortest path to the Glass Citadel." Max, cute and shirtless, the only younger guy she'd had sex with, dead, but not problematically so.

"So, we go that way," Janet said.

Heather knew she was wrong before Max answered, "No. If we make it to the wall, we'll... have help making the journey shorter. We go toward the lake. If you trust my... instincts."

What he *knows*. "Of course," Heather said. She looked at Janet, who nodded. They continued toward the waves and the mists and the shore of Lake Hali.

In Heather's head, rabbits hopped, hunted by the white-gloved hand of The Man in the Grinning Mask. They hopped inside her, and she was a glass house, fragile, ready to break—

but not without surprises.

Max

Max had thought of The Shadow Man as his reflection, and he was, but he was more, too. He was a beacon. The path they followed, no longer a suspended bridge but a trail of cleared land flanked by swaths of dead grass, was the right path because The Shadow Man appeared beside it, at intervals, beckoning.

Heather and Janet didn't see him. The girls engaged in slow-motion chatter about the colors in the sky, the whistling wind, and the whiteness of the wall. They speculated about the Glass Citadel. They accepted without question that they needed to go.

They didn't see him, but Max felt assured of The Shadow Man's presence because he not only encouraged and affirmed their progress, but he brought clarity.

The Shadow Man had been a man, or he would be a man and would become The Shadow Man again. The man's name was Nick, and like Heather, he journeyed with others through The Middle Reaches, and he tried to pass through the Gate. Like

Heather, the Watcher deemed him unfit to pass.

The Mouth tore him apart, and when he joined the dead, as Max joined the dead, he was reassigned. He began to serve. Infinitely isolated, infinitely bound, beholden to Hastur—in service, in death, and with deep, deep cold, he reflected Max, but he had his own memories, or fragments of memories.

Nick remembered a boy named Sheldon. A search for Sheldon brought him through The Middle Reaches, as a search for Bobby brought Max, Heather, and Janet.

Being *already* dead made Max's initial journey different from Nick's, and Max himself made the outcome at the Gate different for Heather. Given leave, The Watcher would have had The Mouth destroy Heather the way it had Nick, but using Max as a conduit, Hastur had intervened for Heather. For what might have been the first time since the Gates came into existence, The Watcher's assessment was overruled.

Why?

Max didn't know.

Max did know other things, however, from gazing across into the white orbs The Shadow Man sometimes used for eyes. Max finally understood the feeling in his stomach. Gordon Marks had stabbed him at the waist and pulled the knife up, up, and up, ripping through his belly. Holding his insides in, Max had fallen on carpet, bleeding to death.

"See you later, Max," Gordon said, and he left Max to die alone, lying on the floor of a house owned by Adam and Ellie Mortimer. Adam Mortimer. The avatar of the God of the Citadel, often Hastur's rival, but now because of the threat posed by Heather's boogeyman, Bobby's boogeyman—The Man in the Grinning Mask—he was Hastur's ally.

Gordon served Adam. If Adam was Hastur's ally, and Hastur was calling Heather to him, why would Gordon and Steven attack them?

Max didn't know, but he did know something he didn't know when, how, or whether to share with Heather and Janet. Gordon, Steven, and Adam would be at the Glass Citadel when they arrived.

"Hurry," The Shadow Man said, his voice a booming whisper.

"Max?" Behind him, Heather tapped his bare shoulder. He looked back but kept walking. Heather asked, "Did you hear...?"

"The wind," Max said. "We have to keep moving." He didn't tell her anything else.

Steven

"It really is a fucking carnival," Gordon said. "Carnival of Meat. Coolest fucking thing I've ever seen."

Gordon didn't sound enthusiastic very often. Steven didn't know how Gordon would react to what... Steven saw. Or didn't see. Or if it was important. Or if he was important. Was he even supposed to be here? Bobby and Sheldon had gone their own way. Gordon hadn't noticed, or he didn't care. Steven noticed. Steven cared. But he didn't say anything.

All the exhibits were... different... but this one was different from the others because all the surfaces weren't glass like aquarium walls. Steven looked in a mirror, reflective but opaque. To his left, black curtains covered a doorway that led to another glass chamber with one mirror surface. Gordon was there now.

"Gordon?" Steven squawked. He needed someone. Bobby had left. He needed his brother.

"What?"

"Could you come out here, please?"

Gordon emerged from the curtains. "What is it?" He came

to Steven's side.

"The mirror," Steven said.

"You... you're not in it," Gordon said. His reflection stood alone.

"Why not, you think?" Steven asked.

"Fuck if I know."

Steven looked at his brother's reflection. He was kind of dirty. Wild hair. Smudged cheeks. Steven didn't remember where he'd put down the hatchet, but he didn't have it anymore. If he had it, he might smash the mirror that refused to reflect him. What might happen to him if he did? He had a direct connection to the King himself. Or at least Gordon did.

"Gordon, do you think I'm nobody?"

"What?" Gordon said. "Stupid question."

"Answer it," Steven said, wincing a little as he realized he'd given Gordon a command.

"You're my brother, at least," Gordon said, turning his head away. "You should get a look at the mirror behind the curtains."

"What'd you see?" Steven asked.

"Want to ruin the surprise?"

"Yes."

"It's like... an X-ray or something, except it shows all your muscles and organs, you know, the meat. All different shades of red and purple, kind of glistening. When you touch different parts of yourself, you get pop-ups. They give you flavor descriptions and recipe recommendations. It's all... funny, in a way, but I guess it could be useful, too, in the right situation." Gordon smirked at Steven, who wasn't sure what "the right situation" would be.

"I'll go," Steven said. He wanted to be brave. He hoped he'd see what his insides looked like, not nothing at all.

He stood in front of the black curtains. He felt afraid to pass through.

"Want me to come with?" Gordon asked.

Yes yes yes yes yes yes! "Yeah, okay," Steven said.

The Marks boys stepped through the black curtains. The chamber was almost too small for them, but they stood side by side in front of the mirror, which reflected Gordon stripped to meat.

At first Steven thought that this mirror was omitting him, too, but Gordon snapped his fingers and pointed toward where Steven's feet should have been reflected. There, twitching its pink nose and whiskers, sat a white furry rabbit with long relaxed ears. It looked up at Steven with quizzical, pink-rimmed eyes.

Gordon patted Steven on the back and said, "Bro, you're a bunny." Gordon laughed, but he stopped himself, maybe because he saw how serious Steven looked. Steven didn't want to be a rabbit. Rabbits were prey. Steven didn't want to be prey. He wanted to be somebody who mattered.

"You're not going to leave me, are you?" Steven asked.

"Let's get out of here," Gordon said, leading them through the black curtains. "And I've got this idea that we work together now, with Adam, as long as he sticks around, but when he doesn't, it's you and me."

"Good," Steven said. "Good."

Janet

They walked the edges of Lost Carcosa to reach the cobalt blue shores of Lake Hali, which they could follow to the border of the Walled City, where, somehow, they would be transported to a castle—no, scratch that, *the* Glass Citadel—where they would finally reach their murky destination. Fiction writing had never really interested Janet, but she wondered if she should change her mind.

"We've been talking," Heather said, "about how strange everything is, but I have this feeling... it's... almost embarrassing...."

"I've got nothing on up top except a bloody bra, and I'm covered with oozing scabs," Janet said. "Little kids who saw me would scream and run away. We're past embarrassing."

"Okay, so *please* tell me if you've felt anything like this," Heather said. She looked forward, at Max's well-formed, bare back. Janet wondered if Heather would have rather been talking to him, but she stayed with her out of pity. If so, that was okay. Janet didn't mind pity right now.

"Okay," Janet said.

"This place is... definitely weird, but... it's sort of... familiar."

Janet could handle that. "Like from your dreams?" she asked.

"Maybe," Heather said. "Familiar might not be the right word, or the only word. On the one hand, I'm as stunned as you are by seemingly random movements in the sky, or the seemingly coordinated movements of the mists on the lake up ahead, or, well everything, but on the other hand...."

Janet really had no idea where Heather was going with this line of thought. "On the other hand?"

Heather's voice quieted: "I almost feel at home here."

Janet did her best not to express any reaction. She couldn't think of a suitable yet honest reply. They walked without speaking. The whistling wind, the humming stars, and the splashing waves of the lake, which got louder and louder, were their background.

At last, Max stopped, turned, and said, "Here the path turns, and we follow the shore. The path gets narrower as we go forward. We'll come close to the water. *Do not touch the water.*"

With his exhortation, Max's brown eyes gleamed yellow, presumably because his God-King spoke through him, which reminded Janet: "So we're being led by a god who can, like, teleport us from the wall to the Glass Citadel, right? Why can't he, since he's a god and all, just teleport us from here?"

"Different areas have different dominions," Max said, "and though no god rules Lost Carcosa, a recent... stirring of ghosts... creates difficulties. When we touch the wall, we make contact with Hastur's domain. Then there are no difficulties."

"In the category of things you know, right Max?" Heather said.

Max's expression changed, as if bright light flashed in his face. "Yeah," he said. "Yes."

They followed the path along the blue shore, and the ruddy water, swirling with the complete spectrum circulating in the sky above, got closer and closer. When they closed to a single file, Janet found herself in the back, watching Heather in front of her almost as much as she watched their reflections in the ebbs and flows of the lake. They were a skin parade. Max's jeans made him the most fully dressed.

The idea of a "skin parade" stuck with her, and she stopped when the water gave her a good look at the skin on her face. Three cuts would scar her there. She was looking at them, thinking of the hag she would be if she lived, when, starting at her hairline, the skin of her face rolled off like wallpaper coming unglued, leaving a bloody mesh exposed to moist air. It was only a reflection. An illusion. But....

She was going to die in the Glass Citadel. It was in the category of things she *knew*.

They reached the wall and placed their hands on it. A second later, they stood in the majestic, open doorway of the Citadel, where the Carnival of Meat had begun.

EPISODE 27: MEAT

Max

Pounding kettle drums and descending arpeggios on what sounded like an electric bass created deeper vibrations than the hum of the black stars—outside? The stars *were* outside, meaning Max and the girls were inside, but looking up, Max could still see the stars and sky through layers of glass that took their images and scattered them, or their ghosts, throughout the Citadel. The glass shook. Max shook.

It was a party.

A short man in a ridiculous red brocaded shirt that ballooned at the shoulders waddled toward where Max, Heather, and Janet stood near the entrance to the Glass Citadel's vast but densely populated welcoming chamber. He broadcast good cheer. Blocking out the room's more insidious activities, Max focused on the man, round belly, stubby legs, pale face makeup like the Elizabethans wore, and wavy orange hair standing up in two points probably supposed to resemble horns, but they looked too silly.

"Welcome, finely dressed young people," the silly man said. The vast chamber's glass walls—difficult to look at because he could see through them while reflected light also repelled his eyes—had decorations. Weapons. Axes, knives, swords, spears, all designed to cut or stab. Nothing like a gun, not even a bludgeon. These decorations split flesh. Some of their configurations looked meaningful.

"Whoo-oop! Whoo-oop!" The sounds came from deeper inside the room, the center, where the attending masses made space for something.

Parts of the crowd cheered. The kettle drums and guitar kept their hammering rhythms.

"Thank you," Heather said. The amazement in her voice had nothing to do with the silly man. She looked directly at what Max didn't want to see.

"Feel free to wear... less. Hm-hm-hm," the silly man said. "We do like young bodies here at the Carnival of Meat."

Max wished he had a jacket to offer Heather. She looked okay, though. Maybe she didn't feel the sickening cold that made his arm hairs stand on end.

Gooseflesh, he thought. *Gooseflesh at the Carnival of Meat.*

"Carnival of Meat?" Heather asked.

"I think I'm going to be sick," Janet said.

"Do you not know?" the silly man said. "Are you not invited?"

"Adam expects us," Max said.

"Pardon me, Adam who?" the silly man said, and Max almost panicked. Instructions weren't popping into his head, but he knew that somehow they had to make it through this... Carnival... and find Adam, or Bobby, or both, and if they couldn't get past this small, round, puffy-shouldered—"Oh! OH!" The silly man lowered his voice. "Not many would know to drop the name of Avin's avatar."

"We're here for Bobby Lightfoot," Heather said.

Max braced himself as the silly man's face became long and serious. "Hm-hm-hm. Are you, now. Then *I* know who *you* are. Heather Park?"

"Whoo-oop! Whoo-oop! Whoo-oop!" The noises—from

some animal—stood out above—everything—and made Max's muscles contract. How many people in the Citadel were actually alive? How many people in the Citadel were actually people?

"Yes," Heather said, rolling her shoulders back defiantly.

"Nice tits," the silly man said. He looked at Max. "You're Hastur's bitch, Max something."

Max didn't say anything. The silly man, his visage softening, glided to Janet, lifted her hand, and kissed it. "You," he said, "are the lovely Janet Fillion. We're so glad you're here."

"Huh?" Janet said. She looked like someone had told her that her big toe had invented nuclear fusion.

"Important guests like yourselves should be on the front row at the arena," the silly man, who didn't seem silly anymore, said. "Follow me. I'll chart a course through the Main Hall."

The not-so-silly man led toward the mass of people and... others... deeper inside the Main Hall, which Max couldn't ignore anymore. What he, Heather, and Janet had done in The Middle Reaches couldn't have been depraved if things like what he saw here could happen.

He assumed that at least some of them were after... pleasure.

Women and men, and those in between or identifiable as neither or both, piled together, sliding against each other, slipping in and out of one another, poking, prodding, squeezing, pinching, twisting—

—cutting, tearing, widening. Cocks, fingers, and tongues moved in and out of newly fashioned orifices, lubricated by spit and blood.

A woman rode a man's erection while holding the end of a cord wrapped around his neck. His face throbbed with trapped blood, and his eyes bulged. His mouth struggled for air but could take in none. She rode on in glee.

A man fucked a woman who lay on her back, which was flat against a bed of nails. With each thrust, the man drove her further down into the bed of nails. Blood dripped from her punctured back, but delight lit up her face. She yelled something Max couldn't hear over the bass and drums.

"Whoo-oop!" Cheers.

A voice, neither masculine nor feminine, shouted through what might have been a megaphone: "YES! Applause, applause! The end must be coming soon!"

The end of what?

Janet stuck closest to the not-so-silly man. The group bundled, staying close as they approached the clearing, the arena that was the source of the cheers and the animal sounds.

Max saw a man and a woman, shoulder to shoulder on their hands and knees, screaming in agony or ecstasy drowned by the bass, drums, and noise of the crowd. Behind them, giant, stone-like creatures with horns and wings—gargoyles? —rammed into them with enormous phalluses. Blood gushed around the stony phalluses' points of entry, but the penetrated didn't resist. They supported themselves as the gargoyles split them from the middle.

"MOVE!" the not-so-silly man commanded, and "people," one of them with a face made of mouths that opened and closed without ceasing, shifted so that Max, Heather, and Janet could stand at the very edge of the clearing that served as an arena where a young man—a kid, really, maybe a year or two younger than Max, wearing a loincloth—fought a thing three times his size that combined bird, scorpion, and... unknown.

The head looked like a chicken's, but with bulbous eyes that had hourglass pupils that rotated as the thing pecked with its elongated, serrated beak, which opened and let out, "Whoo-oop! Whoo-oop!" It skittered on arachnid legs in circles around the boy, who swung and lunged at it with a halberd, scoring hits that seemed to make it angrier.

The boy held the halberd in his left arm. His right arm bled from a place where a chunk seemed to be missing. He hobbled to remain on guard against the creature: his left leg bled from a place where an even bigger chunk seemed to be missing.

A figure dressed like a jester, a joker on a playing card, stood on a platform at one end of the arena and did, in fact, hold a megaphone. "Coming soooooooooon!" the Jester repeated.

"Whoo-oop!" the creature cried, and it dove at the boy, beak opened like pincers. The beak grabbed the boy's neck and tore most of it away in a spray of blood that sent the watching part of the crowd into exaltation, screaming, cheering, applauding.

With rapid pecks, the creature tore more meat from the boy's bones, stripping him.

"Okay," the Jester said through the megaphone. "Let's clear up these leftovers and put the winner in her pen. It's time for the next event."

"Ah, Miss Fillion," the not-so-silly man said, putting his arm around Janet. "We really are so glad to have you here today."

Bobby

He and Sheldon walked so fast that he was wheezing, and he was almost out of breath, but the reflections kept telling them that the gargoyles were getting closer, so they had to keep moving, doing whatever they had to do to keep the creeping reflections at a distance, because if the gargoyles—

and then the music started, and the gargoyles disappeared. The low, thumping notes echoed, but the echoes weren't so confusing that they didn't provide a sense of their origin. Bobby and Sheldon followed them until a hall of mirrors became a glass room, and the glass room led out onto a glass balcony.

The balcony overlooked the Main Hall, the rectangular perimeter of which was easier to discern because the exhibits, mostly bodies *in extremis*, lined the back corners, the huge open door added illumination to the front, and writhing forms packed the space in between, except for a square in the middle with a platform on one side.

The forms nearest the square didn't engage in the same... activities. They watched the blood-spattered square or looked at the platform by one of the square's sides, where a jester stood. The Jester held a megaphone and blasted, "It's time for the next event!"

"I never... never read... never imagined... anything like this," Sheldon said. "It's an orgy. It's the Marquis de Sade."

Bobby had never been to an orgy or read anything by the Marquis de Sade, but writhing forms below looked familiar because he'd seen the ceilings in the halls of mirrors, the images made from mosaics of stained glass. Every orifice or crevasse received any body part that could enter it. Hunger, delight, relish. Bodies lay in pieces, here a leg, there a head. Flaying, dismemberment, pain.

The Main Hall added motion and sound: thrusting, smacking, ripping, moaning, screaming, crying.

Plainer movement turned Bobby's attention to the back of the Hall. He spotted Gordon and Steven weaving through piles of bodies, toward the front of the crowd attending the bloody, vacant square.

Still using the megaphone, but in a confidential tone, the Jester said, "You'll love this."

A commotion on the side of the square opposite Gordon and Steven caught Bobby's eye. Instantly, he recognized two people he hadn't expected to see again. The first was Heather Park, who used to be his babysitter. Seeing her naked on top felt uncomfortable, even with all the flesh bared around her. The other person was Max Gracey, a kid from the neighborhood who went out with Chris's big sister.

Another girl, a white girl with burgundy stripes on her front that might have been scabs, seemed to be with Heather and Max, or was trying to be with Heather and Max. A short, round man with orange spikes of hair had two naked revelers joining him in an effort to drag the girl away, toward the vacancy of the square. Meanwhile, forms from the mass, possibly human, held back Heather and Max.

"No no no no no no!" the girl cried.

"JANET!" Heather screamed. Drums pounded. Low notes descended in threes. Being able to make out individual voices within the din seemed like a miracle.

With hushed excitement, the Jester said through the megaphone, "For the Carnival of Meat's next event, I have the pleasure to welcome to the arena... Miss Janet Fillion!"

The Carnival of Meat.

Bobby heard nothing but the crowd's cheers as the round man and his two helpers deposited Janet at the center of the vacant, blood-spattered glass floor. She folded her arms across her red-stained bra and looked around her. She trembled. Some of her wounds—the places scabbed over—wept.

Miss Janet Fillion was meat.

"We need to get out of here," Sheldon said.

Gordon and Steven Marks might have belonged to Adam Mortimer, but they were still meat. Heather Park was meat. Max Gracey looked... different... but might have been meat. The Carnival of Meat.

"Come on," Sheldon said. "We go. Now."

Bobby and Sheldon were not meat.

"We need to go down there," Bobby said.

"Are you crazy?" Sheldon asked.

Sheldon wasn't in charge anymore.

Gordon

Gordon was getting ready to take off his clothes and jump into a mass of bodies when the voice with the megaphone said, "You'll love this."

In both ears, Gordon heard whispers: *Go to the arena.* He knew what they meant.

"Come on," he said, and he grabbed Steven's wrist. Nobody bothered them as they wound through piles of people (most of them people, anyway) fucking, and some even made room as they shoved their way into the front of the crowd facing the open square.

On the other side were Heather and Max, restrained by partygoers. Other partygoers were dragging Janet into the middle of the square. Gordon smiled and said, "Looks like I don't get to finish the job."

"You think they're going to...." Steven was barely audible over the crowd's growing excitement.

"Let's watch," Gordon said.

Someone dressed as a jester said through the megaphone, "For the Carnival of Meat's next event, I have the pleasure to welcome to the arena... Miss Janet Fillion!"

The crowd, even the orgiastic mass, got quieter when five thick metal chains, spread throughout the arena, fell from the invisible ceiling. At the end of each chain, hooks faced in opposite directions, forming anchor shapes. The part of the crowd watching oohed and aahed.

Janet stood in the square's center, arms crossed over her chest, shaking. She was quiet.

At the edge across from Gordon and Steven, Heather and Max stopped struggling and watched.

"Shhhhhhhh," the Jester said. Even the screaming of the mass's victims faded.

Slowly at first, as if moved by a breeze, the chains and their anchors began to swing. Gordon could tell the direction of Janet's gaze by the movements of her head, but he wished he could look into her eyes as she began to track the anchors' accelerating movements. She unfolded her arms and stepped sideways as one of the anchors came close to her position. Her eyes, too far away for him to see, would confirm whether she knew what Gordon knew.

The anchors hunted her.

The pendulous chains didn't move on parallel or even regular pathways but instead swung on wobbly, wavering lines that could cross anywhere, as if they didn't have a fixed connection wherever they originated above. Janet's first careful sidestep became more steps and more, and she lost the frightened deer look and jogged, charting courses around the hooks' swinging, changing, thrusting pathways.

She only tried to escape into the crowd once, and the result was a shove that almost impaled her. The Jester laughed through the megaphone, and the crowd laughed along.

To dodge, Janet dropped to the glass floor and rolled, but one of the anchors dipped low enough to hit her even lying down, so she got to her feet and jumped, evading by a hair. This girl—this girl he had striped with a razor—could still do so much to preserve herself. Her quick movements, the rolling, the jumping: they had split open most of the stripes. Janet bled from head to toes.

The anchors swung faster, and she moved faster, but she was losing coordination. Soon she would trip or make a wrong move. She had to know that this... show... would go on until she couldn't. She had to know it was her end. Gordon was looking at a person powered by pure survival instinct in the face of certain destruction. It was like one of Adam's personal lectures, but better.

Janet didn't trip, and as far as Gordon could tell, she didn't make a wrong move, either, because suddenly three anchors came at her, and she had no move to make. She dove, but one of the hooks caught her left shoulder and lifted her into the air. She slowed its swing and brought it back down.

When she landed with a scream, hook sticking out of her back, the crowd gave brief applause before the Jester hushed everyone.

With one hook in her, Janet could keep trying to escape the other four. She wasn't trying, though. She pulled at the metal stuck in her shoulder. Did she really think she could remove the hook? She didn't seem to see the anchor swinging toward her. It could plunge directly through her skull—

but she stumbled out of the way, taking her hands from the anchor that her shoulder brought with her, chain rattling above.

Motion on the platform where the Jester stood, and a flash of red that reflected everywhere, made Gordon look away from Janet's amazingly awesome show. Adam! He'd come back from tending to *our special guest* and stood on the platform with the Jester, watching. Adam caught Gordon looking at him, nodded, and waved. Gordon waved back. Being singled out by such a party's host was an honor, right?

When Gordon looked back at Janet, a second anchor had caught her, this time in the right calf, sideways in the back. Janet, hooked on both sides, could still move, dragging chains above her. She got out of one faster-swinging anchor's way, then another's. Gordon felt glad she would die, but he also admired her.

Red slicked her visible skin.

She didn't last long before the third, now fast-swinging anchor caught her, driving a hook through her left hand and pulling it so her arm extended maximally, at a wide angle from her hooked left shoulder.

Held up by taut chains, she stopped moving, but Gordon could hear her whimpering in the quiet Hall.

The fourth anchor hooked her left thigh. The fifth hooked her right arm.

Janet splayed upright, pulled in all directions, a red picture of pain. It was beyond what he, Adam, and Ellie had been capable of back in the world where they'd started. Gordon looked to Adam. Did Janet, strung up on chains, waiting to die, anticipate his future? As long as Adam stayed with him, and with Steven, did he have delights like Janet to look forward to?

Heather

Tenterhooks.

The hooks that held Janet in place—pulling her shoulder up one way, one arm another, the other arm another, one leg another, the other leg another—almost seemed to stretch her out within a three-dimensional frame, like cloth stretched on tenterhooks. Of course, these hooks were double-sided and rounded and punched holes in Janet at least as big around as golf balls—

Heather was about to watch her oldest friend die. She stood in a glass house—she *was* a glass house—watching her friend die.

For a moment, as the crowd stayed silent, the taut chains, with Janet suspended among them, did not move. Then the man in the red shirt on stage

(Avin)

who looked important and familiar

(Adam)

clapped his hands.

A chain twitched, and Janet's left hand twitched. Another chain twitched, and her right arm rose and fell. A chain jumped, and her right knee bent, making her foot stomp the glass floor. Another chain moved, and her left leg rose to the side and fell. A chain spun, and so did she.

All at once, chains moved to the rhythm of the bass and drums, making Janet move with them, their dancing marionette. Some movements were travesties but nonetheless recognizable—plié, sauté, pirouette—and some movements seemed random, a jerk this way or that, a half-spin sliding toward one side of the arena, a half-spin sliding toward the other. On the chains, gravity was mostly irrelevant.

As Janet moved, the hooks tore her, but they didn't pull all the way through her shoulder, calf, hand, thigh, or arm. They kept their holds. She bled and bled, but Heather could see her breathing as she danced and danced, no movement her own. The more she moved, the more... graceful... she seemed.

She took a very long time to die.

Heather felt herself crying.

"It's okay," Max spoke into her ear. "I'll get you out of this."

He didn't understand. Heather was made of glass. She should have been cracking in a million different places.

She couldn't discern the moment of Janet's death, but she knew the dance went on afterward because the chains brought her body close to where Heather stood, and Janet's eyes were lifeless. Afterward, Janet performed a soaring leap and landed in the square's center with a spin.

At last, Janet came to a halt, suspended in the position

that had made Heather think of tenterhooks.

Tentatively, the crowd applauded.

Adam, or Avin, clapped once.

The chains all pulled in different directions, and Janet came unsewn. Her pieces slid off the hooks and scattered on bloody glass.

Tentatively, members of the crowd moved in. To feed.

"I can't stop crying," Heather said.

"It's okay to cry," Max said. "I... can a ghost be in shock?"

He didn't understand. She was crying because Janet's death was so beautiful.

EPISODE 28: RABBITS IN THE HAT

Sheldon

Sheldon had been sent to guide Bobby, even protect him, and now Bobby was leading Sheldon down another hall of mirrors. Bobby followed the sounds of drums and bass arpeggios. The boy got not just a *sense* of direction from them but almost a mental roadmap. He stopped in front of a mirror and determined it was a door leading to stairs going down.

Down to the Main Hall, the Carnival of Meat, where a girl named Janet had just been impaled on hooks, pulled to pieces, and eaten. Sheldon didn't want to admit that he was afraid. He wasn't afraid of death—that ship had sailed—but he was afraid of pain. The Cavern had whispered about tortures in Carcosa that went on and on and on.

Sheldon was afraid, and Bobby was leading them down the stairs to the Main Hall. He had the courage to move toward danger. He...

... he had taken Sheldon's place. That's what the mirrors meant. They didn't mean they were interchangeable, or spiritual twins, or some other bullshit. They meant that Bobby and Sheldon were trading places. All this time, Bobby had been a parasite. Now he was strong, and Sheldon was weak.

Bobby couldn't help it, though. The kid had such good goddamned intentions and was undeniably, irresistibly...

charismatic.

At the bottom of the stairs, Adam Mortimer waited. "Good," he said when they stood face to face. "I was thinking I would have to search for you. Those... mirror halls... make their own decisions. They were a gift, long ago."

Seeing Adam at the Carnival of Meat was like seeing him closer to godhood. The spectacle was inhuman, and it was *his*. Sheldon didn't know what to say.

"What now?" Bobby said.

"I arranged the meeting you wanted," Adam said. "Follow me." The big man moved out of the doorway, into the Main Hall, and Bobby followed. Sheldon wanted to know what meeting Bobby wanted. Sheldon didn't want a meeting. Not here, anyway. They were only passing through, on their way to Hastur —

Except that wasn't true, was it? Bobby had a destiny here. Because Bobby had created The Man in the Grinning Mask, Bobby was central, chosen, essential, and Sheldon was...

inconsequential.

Not far into the Hall, two more pairs of people waited to join them in following Adam. Sheldon felt familiar enough with Gordon and Steven Marks. He disliked them both, not because they were murderers—one couldn't toss around moral judgments here—but because he envied Gordon's relationship with the God of the Citadel and found Steven just inherently unlikeable.

The other pair, Sheldon didn't know. Bobby had identified them as Heather Park and Max Gracey, but he hadn't mentioned that Max was already dead, an interesting omission. Perhaps Bobby didn't know. Perhaps *Max* didn't know. If they were all "meeting" with The Man in the Grinning Mask, they were likely confronting said Man, a hell of a time for Max to start an angsty voyage of post-life self-discovery.

Members of the promiscuous crowd were quick to make room for Adam, so the walk to the back of the Main Hall was direct. In the rear wall's center, between two exhibits (one featured a young man who seemed to have ripped out his own heart and impaled it on a stick, and the other featured a woman whose skin was peeling off and turning into butterflies) was a door. Adam held it open.

"My Audience Chamber," Adam said. "Rarely seen."

They filed in, Adam last, and when the door closed behind them, it disappeared. The Chamber's first impression was freezing cold. Sheldon was shivering before his eyes and brain processed that the room looked nothing like a royal audience chamber, no throne, no red carpet, no decoration of any kind. Stacks of boxes lined the glass walls. In the room's center stood a small, round table, perhaps a pedestal.

Most of the boxes had holes in them as if they had been punctured or... stabbed. Run through.

"We're not in the Glass Citadel anymore," Max said.

"Technically," Adam said, "we are."

"We're not in Carcosa," Bobby said.

"No," Adam said. "This room becomes... detached. It might be easiest to say we're in The Middle Reaches. Middle ground. No one has any... unfair... advantages."

"Not you, and us," Heather said, "and not—"

A feminine voice, loud enough to reverberate off the glass walls but nevertheless soothing, filled the chamber. "I am the Herald of The Man."

Adam folded his arms across his chest, squeezed the bridge of his nose, and shook his head.

"What?" Gordon whispered.

"It's a little ostentatious," Adam said in low tones. Sheldon agreed, but his agreement was irrelevant.

"His coming was foretold," the Herald said.

"Prophecy bullshit," Adam said. "Boring." Gordon laughed.

"An army follows in his wake," the Herald said.

Adam yawned.

The light in the room, wherever it originated, went out. They stood in total darkness, and Sheldon told himself that he could die a million times, and it wouldn't matter. He had things to fear, but death—unending darkness or simply another elsewhere—was not one of them.

Across the room, light appeared as if through parting curtains. The silhouette of a tall, slender figure in a cape and top hat appeared. He held a cane or a... sword... and stepped forward.

Regular light returned to the room. The Man held his narrow sword like a cane, and a breeze from nowhere ruffled his red cape. With his immaculate black suit and white shirt, he wore a black bow tie. The defining feature, the Grinning Mask, was gold, and the grin stretched from ear to ear, almost like a comedy mask, but more slanted, more sinister. Abominable.

The Man in the Grinning Mask stepped up to the table at the room's center, took off his black top hat, and set it upside down as if on a pedestal. He tapped its rim with the tip of his sword, then stepped backward, away from where Sheldon and the others stood. The Man had made an opening gambit of some kind. They were supposed to do something.

Sheldon couldn't do anything. He was worthless.

Heather

She waited for the rabbits because he *was* the nightmare.

Since she'd realized she might meet The Man in the Grinning Mask, she hadn't had much opportunity for considering expectations about his appearance, but she supposed she'd expected to perceive some difference between dream and reality, something that made the dream her own and *him* a true *him*. No. He looked exactly as he did in her dreams, more terrifying than mere appearances should allow.

He flickered.

The black suit, the black bow tie, the red cape, the gold mask—flickered.

In the Main Hall, weapons had lined the walls. Useful things. Here, boxes, many of them in shoddy shape, stood in stacks. The Man in the Grinning Mask had a mean-looking sword, a rapier, if she remembered correctly. She supposed they'd fight back with cardboard.

They did have numbers, but Heather suspected numbers might not matter. They might not matter because—

they were the rabbits. Janet had been meat for the carnival. They were rabbits for the hat. The Man had tapped with his rapier's tip before he had started flickering.

Before Bobby had stepped forward.

The Man in the Grinning Mask was Bobby's nightmare, too. She'd come here, she'd bled, and she'd seen—things—in Bobby's name, but seeing him step forward, she knew Bobby wasn't her reason for being here. Deep beneath the foundation of the glass house, her *self* hid yearning beyond description. First, it had let itself out barely enough to draw her here.

Now, it came further, with crowds of whispers only she could hear. She moved closer to Adam.

The Man in the Grinning Mask, close enough for a sword strike at Bobby, flickered out. His upside-down hat sat alone on the small table, awaiting

(them)

rabbits. The Man in the Grinning Mask was nowhere until

he appeared behind Gordon and slashed between his shoulders. Gordon fell forward and cried out, sounding like a fifteen-year-old boy. Adam caught the boy with one arm and roughly slung him stomach-down across the glass floor—to a safe distance.

"Gordon!" Steven yelled. He ran toward Gordon's new location.

Adam stretched grasping hands toward The Man.

The Man flickered out. Heather looked around. They all looked around, sharing understanding that a Grinning Mask could appear over any of their shoulders at any moment.

Bobby still stood near where The Man had started, near the hat. Max stepped up next to him and held his hand over the hat's vacancy. Were his eyes glowing yellow? Heather couldn't see. She focused between Adam and the entrance, looking at Max's bare back, which must have been as cold as she felt, unless being dead....

Was Max in danger?

Heather looked at Adam. She knew what he had done to Janet, how it had moved her, and she wondered how far his power went. Could Adam, or Avin, make a ghost bleed? Could The Man in the Grinning Mask?

Did these... *higher*... beings know how to kill a ghost?

"Stop," Max said.

Heather heard, "Hm-hm-hm, hm-hm-hm, hm-hm-hm, hm-hm-hm, hm-hm-hm," echo around her, and it sounded familiar, but two words made her recognize the voice of the round man with orange horns of hair who had welcomed them into the Glass Citadel's Main Hall:

"Hastur's bitch."

The Man in the Grinning Mask appeared, solid, behind Max. He shoved the rapier into Max's back until at least a third of it must have protruded through his chest, and then he lifted the sword, and Max with it, into the air.

Max didn't bleed, but he screamed. Hurt. Agony. Ghosts could feel pain. Heather breathed it in. She tasted it.

With a jolt of his arm, The Man dislodged Max from his sword and lobbed him toward the hat. Max should have crushed it, and probably the table with it, but his body went into it as if through a funnel, and he was gone. The profundity of it hit Heather in a wave.

No more Max, no more Janet.

And they were all rabbits, and The Man in the Grinning Mask was flickering again.

Bobby

Adam said the room was detached. Adam said the room was in The Middle Reaches. The room was... Switzerland. Central and intersectional. Neutral? Maybe. More than anything, though, the room was a construct. It was symbolic. Boxes looked like Bobby's own description of four-dimensional realities stabbed by The Man in the Grinning Mask's sword—symbolic.

Being tossed in the hat, like Max, probably symbolized being cast into a foreverdark of The Man in the Grinning Mask's making.

The Man in the Grinning Mask was a magician, pursuing the highest magics, the symbolic magics of total creation and total destruction. It was the magic on the doorway to the Citadel that brought the Walled City into perpetual being. It was the magic that could replace a thing, something of matter and energy that cannot be created or destroyed, with nothing.

The Man in the Grinning Mask was a symbol, but Bobby didn't know what he symbolized. He was a symbol in the way that Adam was an avatar. The Man in the Grinning Mask was, himself, a mask for something greater. Infinities within infinities. Adam had arranged this "meeting," but so far Adam seemed to have no strategy, and none of them seemed capable of fighting The Man, who could pick them off one at a time. Bobby supposedly had some power, but what was it? He didn't know how to make his eyes glow, hold up his hand, and give an order with any hope of success. He didn't know how to teleport around making vicious attacks.

Sheldon yelped, and Bobby turned to look. The Man was in front of him, slashing him above the knees, tearing his jeans and drawing no blood. Still, Sheldon looked at Bobby with pain in his eyes. His knees buckled. He stumbled but didn't fall forward. *Bobby was supposed to do something.*

WHAT? WHAT? WHAT?

He looked at Adam. "You're a god!" he shouted. "Act like one!"

The Man in the Grinning Mask appeared in front of Adam and, with a spin, ripped open his shirt and chest. Adam *did* bleed. He fell backward, landing on his ass.

The room filled with laughter that reminded Bobby of Vincent Price.

Heather laughed, too.

Bobby looked at Steven, who was helping Gordon to his feet. If he were with Steven and Chris in Dimension X, and they were fighting a big bad guy at the end of an adventure, what would he do?

He stomped his foot on the glass floor and shouted, "SHOW YOURSELF AND FIGHT ME, YOU COWARD!"

Heather burst into new, more uproarious laughter.

Sheldon

Sheldon focused all he had on not curling into a crying

ball over the pain in his legs while Bobby called out the demon: "SHOW YOURSELF AND FIGHT ME, YOU COWARD!"

The gash across Gordon's back had looked nasty, wide-open skin where there wasn't much skin to begin with, but Gordon was on his feet, looking for a fight. Adam, too, with his slit chest (granted, his pecs might have served as body armor) was up and ready. "I've had enough of this," Adam said, bleeding chest heaving. "You IMPETUOUS CHILD!"

The Man in the Grinning Man flashed into existence in front of Gordon and Steven, but with his back to them. He thrust his sword behind him, tilted his head left and right, and flashed back out.

"Oh fuck!" Gordon yelled.

Steven collapsed to a sitting position, holding his stomach as blood flowed over his hand. A direct hit, and Steven was alive but would bleed to death. It would take a long time. Stomach wounds were supposed to be painful. So much pain.

The Man in the Grinning Mask was making rounds.

"He's playing goddamned games!" Gordon yelled.

Yes. He would hobble them. Hurt them. Keep hurting them. On and on and on.

Max got off easy. For the living, the meat, the hat might have meant death, dismemberment, all manner of physical horror, but for Max, or for Sheldon, it might be, it *could* be—

a way out. Sheldon was irrelevant now anyway. He no longer cared for the audience with Hastur he'd dreamed of, or about seeing the inside of the Walled City or the Palace, he only wanted—

escape. Was he so terrible?

And if he didn't escape, he'd go out in glory. He stayed vigilant.

The Man in the Grinning Mask flashed into existence in

front of Heather. He didn't swing the sword at her. He brought his masked face close to hers. Sheldon couldn't see their up-close interaction, but he saw her push his black-clad chest away from her. The push didn't qualify as a shove, but it hurled him away, toward the center of the room. Toward the hat on the pedestal, and toward Bobby, who waited.

Sheldon was waiting, too. He ran at Bobby, pushing him out of the way of the regrouping Man in the Grinning Mask, whose coming swing might have beheaded the boy. Sheldon tried shoving The Man into the hat.

He pushed and fell with his own momentum, moving through The Man in the Grinning Mask as he vanished from the spot where he stood. A crushing force surrounded Sheldon's body, and he felt himself drawn inward, inward, and light faded until it snapped out.

He didn't know sight or sound. His skin reported nothing, and he didn't smell or taste, yet he did *feel*. He felt falling. Falling, falling, falling. He didn't think the sensation would ever stop, and he thought it might be the only thing left for him.

Gordon

His back hurt like a son of a bitch, but Steven was hurt worse, and Gordon didn't see any way out of this place. If Adam could open the door, let them out—"Adam!" Gordon called.

"Not now," Adam said, looking around the room. Could he sense The Man in the Grinning Mask when he was invisible? Track him? Adam had to have some kind of power, some way to fight he hadn't revealed yet. Mostly, he looked from Bobby to Heather to Bobby again.

Heather faced Adam. "You'll regret it if you do," she said.

Gordon didn't understand what she was talking about.

"He's afraid of you," Adam said. "He's afraid of *both* of you.

Bobby, you have to fight him."

"I don't know how," Bobby said.

"Children," Adam said. "In the end, always children."

"Adam!" Gordon barked. "Steven needs help! Get us out of here!"

"Not now," Adam said. He stepped toward the boxes stacked against the nearest wall, picked up a box, and weighed it in his arms. "Don't try this at home, kids." He threw the box across the room.

The box soared over the hat and hit the glass floor on the room's opposite side, sliding before coming to a halt. The room quaked.

Heather moved closer to Adam. She had the right idea. Gordon helped Steven halfway to his feet and closed in on Adam, who picked up another box. "I'll hit you sooner or later," Adam said. He threw the box.

The pitch was good, hip-level through the room, but no hit until it crashed into other boxes. A bigger quake. Gordon let Steven slip back to sitting. The blood gushing over the hand on his gut didn't look good.

Adam already had another box. "Here goes," he said, and threw. The box went up and came down in a higher arc, and as it came down, it moved through something like an unstable hologram—The Man in the Grinning Mask, his position revealed. Adam didn't wait. He threw another box, and another, and each one hit The Man, making his image stronger.

As his image got stronger, The Man, Gordon hoped, got weaker.

Adam said, "Gordon!" as he threw another box. He gestured for Gordon to come near, so Gordon did. Adam threw another box—the room's quaking made walking toward Adam difficult—then reached into his pocket. He pulled out a polished brown handle that Gordon recognized. He threw another box while handing it over. "In case you need it."

Gordon accepted the straight razor, and Adam carried a box as he moved toward The Man. He hit The Man squarely in the head, and the box fell between them. As the room quaked, Adam lunged and pressed hands on the sides of The Man's bare-skull head, just beyond the Grinning Mask. With a quick jerk, he twisted The Man's neck in a half-circle.

The crack of the breaking neck filled the room. The Man collapsed to the glass floor in a pile of red cape.

Gordon moved toward Adam's side to get a closer look. The sword seemed to be missing. The *Man* seemed to be missing. He had disappeared, leaving behind his cape.

He reappeared, skinny man in a black suit, between Adam and Gordon. Adam spun toward him, but The Man in the Grinning Mask was fast. With a slash and a jab, he slit Adam's throat and rammed the blade into his chest. As The Man pulled out the sword, Adam dropped to his knees, clutching at his throat, which bled like people bleed. Adam fell forward on his face, in an expanding puddle. He did not move.

"What?" Gordon said. He glanced at Steven, whose drooping eyelids suggested ebbing consciousness. "No!" Gordon said.

Heather kneeled at the edge of the expanding puddle. She put her hand in it and smiled at the red her hand brought back.

"NO!" Gordon shouted.

Heather sighed and exhaled a lazy, "Yes."

Gordon opened the razor. He might not be able to kill The Man in the Grinning Mask, but he *could* kill her.

Steven

Heather looked at the hand she'd covered in Adam's blood. In a sing-song way, she said, "Rabbits in the hat, rabbits in the hat. We don't know who's next when we're rabbits in the hat."

Steven wasn't thinking clearly, but he was pretty sure Heather had lost her fucking mind.

Gordon moved toward her with the razor open, and Steven wanted to warn him that The Man in the Grinning Mask was still there, between Adam's body and the hat. He hadn't... flickered out... he'd stayed. He was close to Heather, close to where Gordon was going. Steven wanted to warn him, but he couldn't catch enough breath to speak. *Please, Gordon. Don't leave me.*

Bobby could have warned him. Bobby didn't say anything.

"You rotten bitch," Gordon said. "I want to cut your tits off, you rotten bitch."

Gordon was right. With Max and Janet gone, Heather was the only one left to blame. They'd gone after her, again and again, and she had only brought grief. They'd followed Bobby and Sheldon, too—Sheldon wasn't part of the picture anymore —but they weren't really *after* Bobby. They were *after* Heather. Why? Why was killing her so important if they all turned out to be on the same side?

He would have asked Adam, but Adam was dead. Had The Man in the Grinning Mask really killed a god?

Gordon got closer to Heather, and The Man in the Grinning Mask got closer to Gordon. Steven couldn't call out to his brother, but maybe... maybe he could stand. The pain was less now. His vision was blurry, his balance weak, but he got to his feet.

Gordon looked ready to swing the razor at Heather, but he feinted and turned on The Man, arcing toward the exposed bit of neck above the black bow tie. The blade got stuck. No blood.

The Man picked up Gordon and threw him in the hat.

Steven, unsteady, stumbled toward the hat. He might have heard Bobby yelling for him to stop. He wouldn't stop, though. He followed his brother now. He fell into the hat, and he kept falling.

EPISODE 29: NO MASK

Bobby

Steven Marks had fallen into a rift in time and space.

Bobby faced the hat, upside-down on its pedestal. Like the punctures in the boxes that stood for holes in, the new porousness of, realities, the hat was a symbol, a representation of a rift that devoured. It was a special rift, this foreverdark of The Man in the Grinning Mask's making. It fed The Man as The Man fed it. Bobby could tell. He could feel The Man getting stronger.

Max fell in. Stronger. Sheldon fell in. Stronger. Gordon fell in. Stronger. Steven...

The Man. Strong enough to kill a ghost? Strong enough to kill a god?

What *was* he?

His coming was foretold.

Yes, and?

An army follows in his wake.

A champion. A first wave. At war against the gods. At war against existence.

Bobby sensed movement behind him. He glanced at Heather, who watched, then focused on the hat, thinking of Steven.

Behind him, The Man in the Grinning Mask raised his

sword.

Bobby could follow Steven into the dark.

The Man thrust at him, and he dove out of the way. He landed on his belly in the puddle of Adam's blood still spreading over the glass floor. Quickly, he flipped onto his back, battering himself in red, and watched for The Man to follow up on the advantage, to make a killing strike—

but The Man disappeared. "COWARD!" Bobby screamed. Bobby wanted a fight. He didn't know how he could possibly stand up to *him*, but he wanted a fight, and his scream came out of pure hate. Steven, gone. Sheldon, gone. Eaten by the rift that fed whatever hid *behind* the Grinning Mask. The coward. Why even call him The Man when a man was precisely what he wasn't? A force, maybe, but not a man.

Bobby got to his feet, covered in Adam's blood. Close to the entrance, Heather looked at him with a strange expression, tittering. "I dreamed about him, too, you know," she said. "After you... introduced him. I dreamed about him, too. I think I might have dreamed," and she looked around the room, "about this meeting." Her laugh became louder, but it cracked with shivering.

Bobby had forgotten the cold. Heather, wearing only shorts, was freezing. He at least had a shirt on, but he was freezing, too, and now he was wet. Wet and alone. Heather wasn't *with* him. Her mind hardly seemed to be there at all. Why had she come? How had she survived?

"Did you happen to notice," Heather said, "that when Max got skewered, he didn't bleed?"

Heather wasn't gone, but she was... absent. Bobby was alone. He'd even left Thing One and Thing Two behind as he'd followed Adam to the Audience Chamber, forgetting them like he'd forgotten the cold, too caught up in the moment.

Steven was gone. He'd loved Steven.

Sheldon was gone. He'd loved Sheldon, too.

He wouldn't forget. He was going to kill The Man in the Grinning Mask. A second time, Bobby filled the glass room with his voice: "SHOW YOURSELF AND FIGHT ME, YOU COWARD!"

Heather

Maybe all the rabbits were in the hat. Maybe she and Bobby weren't rabbits. Maybe being made of glass, like the Citadel, set her apart. Or maybe what set her apart was the yearning she felt in her chest and stomach, not her own, certainly not Bobby's or The Man's—it radiated to her extremities.

Bobby covered in Adam's blood made her laugh. She found lots of things funny now. The Grinning Mask, a comedy mask. The Man stepping out from between parted curtains. Showmanship! It was all a show, a comedy. She laughed harder.

When Bobby repeated his heroic "show yourself" line, she didn't find it as funny. She hadn't decided whether she wanted to see the boy live or die. He'd never seemed particularly brave when she'd been his babysitter, but he was courageous now. That made him worth watching. But what The Man in the Grinning Mask might do to him—

maybe like Janet on tenterhooks—

could be worth watching as well.

She became so focused on watching for The Man to attack Bobby that she almost didn't notice him materialize in front of her. Like before, he brought himself close to her. Reflected on the golden mask's surface, Heather could see a distortion of her visage, eyes changed, the irises, normally brown, now yellow.

Pulling her attention away from her own eyes, she looked into the holes the mask had for eyes and saw no other eyes behind them, only dark. Inside the mask's wide grin, she saw no other mouth, only dark.

The Man in the Grinning Mask backed away from her and lifted his sword at his side, as if with one swoop at her middle he would cut her in half. "You won't," she said.

The arm raised with the sword, clad in the sleeve of his formal black jacket, struggled.

"You can't," Heather said.

Bobby called from behind The Man, "Heather!"

Heather didn't care. With a smirk, she said to The Man, "You, sir, should unmask."

Indeed?

"Indeed it's time," she said. "We all have laid aside disguise but you."

I wear no mask.

The declaration's truth felt both obvious and horrifying. "No mask?" Heather said. "No mask!"

"Heather, run!"

Heather stepped toward The Man and pressed a hand against the golden face with the permanent grin. Her fingers told her what she already knew: the mask that was not one was made of glass.

Like her.

She heard echoes like she'd heard before: "Hm-hm-hm, hm-hm-hm, hm-hm-hm, hm-hm-hm, hm-hm-hm," the voice of the round man with orange horns of hair from the Main Hall.

Hastur's bitch.

The need to laugh felt stronger than ever. Hysteria welled up to her throat, and she let it explode as she stepped back, pointing at the skinny, tall figure in the black suit. "No mask!" she said, laughing. "No mask!"

The figure with no mask swung the sword.

Bobby

The Thing in the Grinning Mask appeared in front of Heather and raised its sword. Bobby braced himself to watch her die, but The Thing froze. Heather spoke familiar lines and looked as if The Thing responded, but if it did, it was too quiet. By the time Heather cried out "No mask!," Bobby had placed the lines: *The King in Yellow* by Robert W. Chambers.

Carcosa, The Man in the Grinning Mask, what they knew about the King in Yellow—they didn't come directly from Chambers or any one author or from Bobby's imagination or Sheldon's or anyone's, not entirely, but still recitation of the lines from Chambers might have been an incantation. With it, The Man in the Grinning Mask was undone, no longer a man and no longer in a mask. It was a misnomer. An error of creation. Revealed as such, it was primed to be erased.

The Thing swung its sword at Heather, and Bobby was ready. He caught the sword's blade in his bare hands. If he had been alive, the sword would have sliced through his flesh, cleaving his hands' brittle bones. *Did you happen to notice that when Max got skewered, he didn't bleed?* Bobby's hands hurt like hell, but he didn't bleed, and he didn't break. He held the sword tightly, stopping its swing.

The Thing holding the sword turned to him. It tugged the sword but couldn't break his grip. Bobby said, "I'll never be afraid of you again." The Thing pulled. Bobby didn't budge. "You'll fear me, but not for long." The Thing pulled, and Bobby jerked the sword's blade to one side, ripping it from The Thing's hands. A second later, Bobby held the hilt, and he swung—

but The Thing had already vanished. "You'll lose!" Bobby shouted as he started a circuit around the room, swinging the sword at empty—potentially occupied—cold air. Heather

181

covered her mouth and kept laughing.

Maneuvering around the boxes Adam had thrown, realities cast asunder, Bobby hunted. The sword was heavier than it looked, but it still felt natural in his hand, like an extension of his swinging arm. He, Steven, and Chris had used sticks as swords plenty of times in Dimension X. Play. Make-believe. Why should now be any different? Killing The Thing, not a man, not masked, would be...

...always children...

child's play. One last goodbye to childhood.

He came to the hat, upside-down on the small table in the room's center. The hat's opening, fit for a skull, consumed people whole. A rift in time and space. A room full of closed boxes into which this Thing... this magician... had punched holes, a room full of rifts surrounded him. In a place detached from place, he stood amidst tatters of spacetime. Unlike the boxes, the hat was open. It was also pristine.

Bobby rammed the sword through the hat. The sword's tip made a hole as it entered and another as it exited, holes reinforced as Bobby withdrew the sword.

The room quaked. Glass rattled. Freezing air moved toward the hat like water circling down a drain. A jarring, nerve-jangling, high-pitched screech rang out: *EEEEEEEEEEEEEEEEEEEEEEEEEEE—*

and the magician with no mask, no hat, and no cape appeared behind Bobby, reaching for him with gloved hands.

Bobby spun, sword raised. The blade passed through neck as if it were nothing. The razor that had been stuck there fell to the floor. The magician's head, severed, fell to the glass floor, bounced, and rolled until the golden face pointed upward. The body collapsed.

The quaking and screeching stopped, but air kept circling, draining toward the ruined hat.

Bobby walked toward the severed head, punching holes in the fallen body as he moved. He kicked the head. It slid toward Heather. Bobby closed and pocketed the straight razor.

Heather

In a glimmer, in a glamour, Heather saw Bobby—or maybe Robert?—standing by the defeated body of the one they had called The Man in the Grinning Mask, but he was at least ten years older, with stubble to match his thick brown hair stirred by the cold wind. Brawn stretched his white shirt. He had a narrow waist and a different sword, not a rapier but a scimitar, thick curved blade sharp and dripping.

He has been to the other side of madness.

And then he was a boy again, and he kicked the severed head with the golden glass face toward her.

In the end, he... it... was fragile. Made of glass. Like everything around them. Like her.

In a glimmer, in a glamour, she saw herself, a glass house, and she stood inside herself, and the figure with no mask kneeled in front of her. People, along with those who were... less so, would kneel to her. She would become accustomed.

She and the figure that wore no mask were the same except for one crucial difference. The decapitated figure *was* a mask. When, in its fragility, it shattered, it would be no more. She, on the other hand, was more, more than she'd ever imagined. When she shattered, truly broke, she would be free.

She remembered Sheldon's bare feet falling into the hat. Why hadn't the kid worn *shoes?*

Stepping forward, she stomped on the decapitated head, the golden glass face, with a shod foot. The head gave way with an unimpressive crunch, breaking to bits as Heather pushed her shoe onto the sturdier glass floor beneath it. When she pulled her foot back, the head finished caving in, a mixture of glass fragments colored gold, white, and black. They didn't sparkle.

The wind picked up. Bobby looked with amazement at the pulverized glass head, and the wind picked up.

"Is he... dead?" Bobby asked.

More than dead, she wanted to say, *it is null,* but what took her was more than a glimmer, more than a glamour—a trance, a transposition.

In the distance, she heard Bobby's voice: "We need to find a way out of here."

She floated on an ocean, her face to the sky. The massive waves lifted her as high as the spires of the Citadel, then dipped her low as the depths of Hali. She felt disoriented, but she felt peace, peace in looking at the sky.

The slow-moving shape drifting above her blocked out most of the purple with black stars. It was mostly yellow, and it was regal, with a protrusion atop what seemed to be its head that could have been a crown and parts that flowed around its middle that suggested a fine robe. It all seemed alive, however; every squirming bit of it was animate.

He lived.

She felt alive, more alive and *cleaner* than she'd felt since... for as long as she could remember, and her mind was almost expansive enough to take in the details of the shapes within his shapes, the spotted, bulbous connections between islands of twisted flesh that might have served as limbs, the clusters of flowing threads that could have been tentacles, the spiny openings that looked like mouths, the many, many, differently curved eyes.

Far, far away: "Heather, are you okay?"

She breathed him in, and she tried not to cry out as she had a spontaneous orgasm. Air stronger than The Middle

Reaches'—air responding to his will as she rose and fell with the waves.

The pull, the tension, the yearning in her chest and stomach were hot, burning, thawing the cold of the room where —

softly, "HEATHER!!!"—

where she knew she should still stand with the children who needed her with the key to getting out if she only said—

"BREAK ME!"

Her voice carried over the rolling of the waves. *He* heard. The floating juggernaut who had many forms and many faces, the High King—*he* heard, and he accepted her invitation.

A bulbous appendage that might as well have been a hammer descended from the floating yellow body and smashed into the roof of Heather's glass house. Heather stood inside, watching it come down. Like the decapitated head with the golden glass face, the glass house shattered, but it made a glorious sound, cracking and snapping and tinkling and crashing with a shower of shards.

You're free. Come. Meet me.

"HEATHER!!! PLEASE!!!"

Bobby's hands were on her shoulders. He jostled her, the look on his face explaining he didn't know what else to do other than hope she'd snap out of whatever spell she was under. While this life came more fully into focus, she said, "I'm here, Bobby. I'm here."

"We've got to get out of here," Bobby said. "The wind is racing like it'll be a cyclone. It'll pull us into the hat. It might pull everything into the hat."

"No," Heather said. "It won't."

Bobby cried out, "What are you doing?!" as she approached the hat. She thought of Max holding out his hand

and speaking commands as she held her hand over the hat.

"Break," she said.

The room's glass walls exploded, pelting them with tiny glass fragments. At once, the room reattached to the Glass Citadel, again in Carcosa, as the wind stopped and a shockwave spread from the Audience Chamber into the Main Hall, where the atrocity exhibition continued, where revelers still practiced myriad violations, and where the Jester conducted new horrors in the arena.

The force of the blast destroyed the exhibition tanks and caused most of the bodies on display to fall apart. A wall of sharp glass shards, daggers fiercer than the fragments that had hit Heather and Bobby, slammed into the revelers, shredding many while some cowered and tried to flee. Heather moved closer to the Main Hall to take in the lovely chaos.

The wave of force moved upward, taking out uncounted glass ceilings, causing heavy glass rain. The screaming became louder than the breaking.

Following no logic, the floors in the Audience Chamber and the Main Hall did not shatter. They cracked, and pieces fell away into what seemed like emptiness beneath. Heather and Bobby stood on an island of glass suspended by unknown means. At the center of the room, the small table supporting the upside-down hat had its own island.

In the Main Hall, not everyone was as fortunate. Floor crumbled, and revelers fell screaming. Heather couldn't be certain, but she thought the entire arena might have given way. The megaphone magnified the Jester's descending cries for help.

She turned her attention to the Audience Chamber. Bobby studied the floor, probably looking for a path along islands of glass through the Main Hall to the front door, the only way out they knew. That wouldn't suffice. They needed better. Her eyes fell toward Adam's body—which was gone. Glass covered with his blood remained, but his body was gone.

"Is the whole Citadel going to break?" Bobby appeared desperate.

Suddenly Heather knew, knew in the way Max sometimes *knew*, and she answered, "No. The show is merely over." Heather walked to the tip of the glass island she shared with Bobby and, before Bobby could object, jumped to the center island with the table and hat. She pushed the table into a nearby opening in the floor. The hat fell, too, doing nothing else remarkable.

Bobby asked, "What..." but he came closer as he asked, and when he got close enough, he answered his own question by seeing what had been waiting beneath the table: a narrow shaft, going straight down, with a ladder. It was stone, not glass. Something filled the whole shaft with light.

"It leads into the Walled City, doesn't it," Bobby said. He wasn't asking.

"It's the way to go," Heather said. She laughed. "It's why I'm here." She put a hand on her belly. She understood now. She had a purpose.

Bobby

Bobby was scavenging the sheath from the dead magician's body and working up the nerve to go first down the ladder when he heard, near what had been the entrance to the Audience Chamber: *woof-woof-woof-woof-woof-woof-woof*.

He would have forgotten them again, but they hadn't forgotten him. Thing One and Thing Two, with glass fragments visible in their iridescent yellow fur, stood on an island looking at him, jaws lolling, rows and rows of teeth showing, drool dangling, and they were... adorable.

But they couldn't climb a ladder, and they probably wouldn't fit into the shaft. Bobby was already worried about feeling claustrophobic.

Before he realized what he was doing, he'd made the two jumps and was close to the uber-dogs. Heather said, "We should go. Others will come. Go and come, and come and go." She sighed and giggled.

Bobby scratched both uber-dogs behinds the ears, and he gave their backs rough pets, ignoring the glass when it rubbed against his hands. "You're good... um, dogs. Yes, you are."

They whimpered. They understood what was happening. They were smarter than regular dogs. Bobby thought they might understand when he said, "Thank you." He kissed the scar on Thing One's nose.

Bobby returned to Heather and said, "Sorry for making you wait."

"*He* is waiting. We have a meeting," Heather said.

"He," Bobby said. "Hastur. The King in Yellow. The God of the Palace."

Heather giggled. Bobby finished attaching the sword and sheath to two belt loops on his shorts and, telling himself that he was only doing the inevitable, started lowering himself down the ladder. Heather soon followed, and he was looking up at her when he saw Thing One and Thing Two looking down into the shaft at him.

Bobby's heart was breaking until a noise stole the uber-dogs' attention: someone else had come into the Audience Chamber. They growled. They barked. They disappeared, and Bobby felt pretty sure he heard them attack. That was their purpose now. Guarding Bobby's and Heather's escape.

Halfway down the ladder, Bobby's arms and calves hurt. At the bottom, he felt exhausted, but he knew they wouldn't stop. They might never stop.

Heather got to the bottom and said, "Why don't we stop

for a little while? We haven't taken a break since we watched all our friends die and then saved the universe."

Bobby laughed. Maybe Heather hadn't lost her mind after all.

At the bottom of the shaft was a small stone room with one exit, an open doorway into a stone passage going in one direction. Whatever lit the shaft lit the room, but gazing into the passage revealed darkness not too far away. Their destination was there, somewhere beyond the dark.

They sat and leaned against the stone wall. Bobby had to adjust the sheath to lower his left leg.

"Nice rapier, huh," Heather said.

"Seemed like it could be handy," Bobby said. *Rapier*. He'd remember that.

"Maybe you'll need it," Heather said. "Maybe it's why we had to fight him."

We. Had Bobby killed him, or had Heather? "Maybe that's why," Bobby said. He thought about Steven and Sheldon, and he thought, *it has to be about more than a sword*.

"What do you think it is about?" Heather said. "Or was. He who was until recently called The Man in the Grinning Mask. Other than terrorizing us for years, of course."

"I don't know for sure," Bobby said. He grunted, rolling his eyes. "His coming *was* foretold."

"Yeah," Heather said. "An army follows in his wake."

The challenger comes, and we organize! We will march, the Army of Ghosts! We will punish Hastur and—

"The Army of Ghosts," Bobby said.

"Hmmmm?"

"The magician did a lot of damage. He tore lots of openings between realities that shouldn't be there, places where... all kinds of things... could get through. We stopped him, but that doesn't undo what he did." Bobby thought for a moment. "I should probably tell you that... I'm not... technically... alive."

"Don't worry," Heather said. "I'm used to it."

They laughed. Maybe they were both out of their minds. Maybe Bobby didn't care.

EPISODE 30: REPAST

Max

He lay in the dirt. Where the hell was he? The trees, the bushes, the briars, the scent of honeysuckle—the babbling of the creek nearby—he knew where he was. He was in the area between the two unconnected streets called Acton Way.

Why was he here, lying in the dirt? How did he get here?

In his chest, he felt a pinch that went all the way through to his back. He lay face up, so his hand went to the spot above his solar plexus—and found the fabric of his black t-shirt, no hole, no wound, no cause for alarm.

Warm spring air, bright blue sky, fluffy white clouds. No alarms and no surprises.

That song by Radiohead was playing in his mind. Annie liked even older, so-called "classic" rock. She was dead now. Gordon Marks had killed her. That was okay. Gordon Marks had killed him, too.

No alarms...

Max finished letting his eyes soak in the sky's delicious blue before he rolled onto his side and saw something that was *almost* a surprise, except it fit somehow. A blanket. It had a pattern of big pink and white checks, simulating a quilt, but it was a blanket. A *picnic* blanket, closer to the creek.

He got to his feet so he could investigate. The pinching sensation was an afterthought. He felt *good*.

On the blanket, he found a nasty tangle of used plastic wrap near a basket with individually wrapped sandwiches inside. They looked like they were made with that long French bread. Crouching for closer examination, Max saw bacon, ham, turkey, and some kind of fancy cheese. He felt hollowness in his stomach, but it was different from the hollowness he was used to.

He was hungry! He felt like he'd gone years without eating, or wanting to eat, but now—

Not far from the basket, which was half-full of the swanky club sandwiches, Max spotted a tin stocked with chocolate-chocolate chip cookies. Next to that was an unopened bag of potato chips—the good kind, kettle chips. An opened bag lay nearby, and a third bag, also opened, sat by the border of the blanket farthest from the basket.

Max imagined a trail of ants connecting the two potato chip depots, but he didn't see any. He didn't see bugs anywhere. Didn't hear them, either. Other than the babbling creek, the place was quiet.

No alarms...

Max had liked the Radiohead song, "No Surprises," because it was about how suffocating a quiet life in the suburbs, his life, really was, but now he liked the quiet. He'd had enough surprises, but he had also learned that he did not belong to himself. What would come, would come, surprising or not. Blue skies would not last forever.

Sandwiches, chips, and cookies. Whoever had left the picnic supplies had also left a bowl of ripe but unspoiled grapes. Max also thanked the benefactors for leaving plastic cups for consuming the—maybe a little weak-looking—lemonade leftover in the gallon jugs.

He thought of starting with a cookie, but he had a feeling he should pour a drink first.

Janet

She remembered the faces around her in the arena, cheering for her to die. She remembered her body moving, dancing, making her feel more and more exposed to those faces, some of which were at best distantly related to humanity. She remembered ceasing to be whole. She saw herself in pieces. She understood herself *as* pieces.

But now, she was whole. No scabs, no bandages. She was like the girl she had been on the morning she'd followed Heather and Max...

...*here*. She wore the same shorts and shirt, and she felt as good as she had that morning, better, even, because then she'd already started to feel the anxiety that would turn into dread that would turn into fact.

Fact. She was dead, wasn't she?

Did it matter? She was *whole* again. She didn't hurt, except maybe in the most residual way.

She knew the one who had done this to her, who had pulled her strings until he pulled her apart. He had even pulled the strings of Gordon Marks when he had used the razor. Adam, or Avin, the God of the Citadel. She also knew Avin would call her back when he next hosted a Carnival of Meat. She became whole to be scattered again. She *knew*. She also knew she would not dangle on strings forever.

For now, she had the blue sky and the white clouds. With a deep breath, she enjoyed wholeness.

Nearby, movement: she turned and saw Max, shuffling around in what looked like a picnic.

She smiled and called, "Max!" She didn't know why she felt so happy to see him.

Max held a cup, which he lowered as he smiled at her, but

his expression quickly faded to puzzlement. He said, "Janet?"

She ran up and hugged him, sloshing his drink. They'd been intimate. A hug seemed appropriate.

"Janet!" Max said.

She pulled back from the hug and said, "I don't know why I thought I'd never see you again. Did you do all this?" She gestured at the picnic.

"No," Max said. "I... I only just got here and... found it all. It can't have been here long. Whoever left it liked a lot of booze in their lemonade."

"Oh, I could totally have a drink!" Janet said. "But first—guess what?"

Max still looked puzzled. "Okay. What?"

"I'm dead now, too," she said, broadening her smile.

"I think I knew that," Max said.

She crossed the blanket and helped herself to a plastic cup and lemonade. Max was right. Strong stuff. After a couple of gulps, she turned to her erstwhile guide and said, "I don't suppose you know about... Heather?"

"I don't know," he said. "Not for sure."

"But you think you know something," Janet said.

"I think she's still alive," Max said. "Still alive and still... going."

Going. They'd been *going* since Max had shown up at Heather's door. "I want you to know," Janet said, taking a drink, "that I don't blame you."

"Thanks," Max said, mirroring her gulp. "Blame me for what?"

"I *could* blame you for leading us into this, getting me killed, getting Heather lost in another... reality, dimension, whatever Carcosa is. But I don't," Janet said.

"Great," Max said. "I'm glad."

"Do you want one of those cookies?" Janet asked. "I'm dying to try one of those cookies."

Gordon

Gordon knew where they were. It was the clearing near the two dead ends, the meeting of the two Acton Ways, the street where he and Steven lived and the street where the Mortimers lived. Except none of them lived around here anymore. Did they live in The Middle Reaches? In Carcosa? Anywhere? He'd need a place to sleep, if he ever needed sleep, but otherwise he didn't need a home, really.

He didn't know how homelessness would affect Steven. Steven could be so sullen sometimes. He was sensitive. That was okay, though. Steven had to be okay. When Steven was stabbed and bleeding out, Gordon hadn't liked it at all, so he understood Steven had to be okay. They were brothers, and they were a pair, and that was the way it was. Gordon and Steven Marks.

"Gordon, I—"

Gordon put a hand over Steven's mouth, turned him, and pointed through the bushes toward where Max and the girl who'd been ripped apart with hooks and chains, Janet, sat on a picnic blanket by the creek. Their backs were to the bushes, and they were talking and laughing, so they probably wouldn't notice the new arrivals. They looked good for dead people. He didn't want to attract their attention. Yet.

"Just keep it quiet," he told his brother. Steven nodded, and Gordon turned away from the happy picnickers, looking toward the back side of the Mortimers' house, the stairs going up to the deck, the sliding glass doors that led into the kitchen. How odd that when he'd met Adam, that had been Adam's home, strangely fitting for him and his wife, so different from the grandiosity of the Glass Citadel.

"Do you think he's alive?" Gordon asked in hushed tones.

With similar quiet, Steven said, "You mean Adam."

"Adam, Avin, whatever we should call him."

"I don't think he ever liked me," Steven said. "He might have... adopted me, but he didn't like me."

"I think Adam has motives, not feelings," Gordon said. "Still, I think we'd be better off if we were still with him. I don't want to go back to the random shuffle."

Steven chuckled. "Yeah. I don't like all the... in and out. Why, do you think? All that skipping around."

"I figure," Gordon said, and he stopped to think. He hadn't figured anything, but an idea occurred to him, and it made sense. "Adam, or Avin, and the other one, Hastur, were supposed to be teaming up with each other against The Man in the Grinning Mask, but they don't get along. I think maybe, since we worked for one of them, we were supposed to work for both, but since they weren't actually working together all the time, we got scrambled."

"The problem was Heather," Steven said.

"Yeah," Gordon said. "Fucking bitch. And maybe some of it... some of it was to get us ready. Adam doesn't die. Not that easy."

Steven

Steven wasn't sleepy-tired, but he was exhausted, and he didn't want to keep thinking about Adam, or Avin, and Hastur, and Carcosa, and all the *shit* he had been through. He'd gotten Bobby back and lost him again, but that wasn't worth thinking about because Bobby didn't care about him anymore. All Steven had left was Gordon, and he and Gordon were under a beautiful, natural blue sky, and ten yards away...

...ten yards away, people were laughing and eating some sort of chocolate cookies that made his mouth water despite everything he'd seen and done. Sitting on a picnic blanket and chowing down sounded more divine than any entity in a Glass Citadel or Walled City could ever be.

Steven could sense, however, that he and his brother might face some social impediments if and when they tried to join the company of Max and Janet.

Gordon had killed Max. Steven's older brother had stabbed Max in the stomach and lengthened the wound nearly to the point of evisceration, after which he had left Max to bleed to death on the Mortimers' floor. Steven was not skillful in social situations—middle school was a bear—but asking your murder victim to share his cookies seemed awkward at best.

And then there was Janet. Gordon hadn't killed Janet, but he had sliced her up and down with the straight razor, which seemed almost as bad. She probably didn't have warm fuzzy feelings toward Gordon and Steven Marks. Gordon and Steven Marks. Whatever Gordon did kind of leeched into him, didn't it?

"Avin and Hastur, working together, working behind each other's backs," Gordon was saying. Steven tried to pay attention. "Do you know what that is?"

Steven shook his head. He wasn't sure what Gordon was talking about.

"Politics," Gordon said. "We are parts of the timeless clockwork. I fucking hate History class."

Politics. Steven wasn't too young to understand a little about politics. "I'm going," he said.

"What?" Gordon said.

"Politics," he said, and he walked around the bushes, toward the picnic blanket. He stopped with a foot on the blanket's corner. Max and Janet kept talking, not sensing him. He looked back. Gordon had stepped out from behind the bushes, but he hadn't approached. "Um, excuse me," Steven said, voice raised.

Silenced, Max and Janet turned and froze. A potato chip was on its way to Max's mouth. Janet had a handful of grapes.

"Hi," Steven said. Max made eye contact with him, then looked behind him. Janet only looked behind him. "Um, you probably remember I'm Steven."

"Yes," Max said. "We remember." He didn't look scared. That was good.

"That's my brother Gordon back there," Steven said, feeling like a total asshole. "You probably remember him, too." Yeah. Probably. "You probably aren't too happy to see us." Duh.

"What do you want?" Janet said. She wasn't mean about it. She had a right to be mean.

Gordon came to Steven's side. "We don't want to hurt anybody." He huffed and grinned. "Not today."

Max hummed a few notes of a song that Steven couldn't place. He needed something to say and couldn't think of anything. "What's in the basket?" popped out.

"Sandwiches," Max said.

"Enough to share?" Steven asked.

"You want a sandwich?" Janet asked.

"Could Gordon and I sit with you?" Steven asked.

"You want to sit with us," Janet said.

"We were together," Steven said. "On the same side, sort of."

Janet sighed, reached into the basket, pulled out two sandwiches, and held them up abruptly. A pause. "Well, come on!" she snapped. "Steven. You, too, Gordon. Get your butts over here and join the picnic."

Sheldon

His reflection in the creek was his reflection. He saw nobody else, only the boy in the blue-and-white striped polo shirt. Looking down, he saw his bare feet. Still no shoes. The Middle Reaches had a sense of humor.

He was a joke.

Under the bright blue sky, he walked against the current, toward the gathering of people he recognized well enough to guess that they had no business being together.

He was a joke *now* because *then*, whenever that had been, he had been important. When Nick and Leslie had come for him in the Cavern, when they'd set out with Ambrose, Celia, and Pedro to discover what had happened to him, he had been important.

When, in his friends' imaginations, he had been the architect of The Middle Reaches and Carcosa, he had been important.

He had felt important, and after he'd become part of The Middle Reaches and learned more about the gods he'd thought he'd invented, he'd imagined a greater destiny, being a servant of two masters, one of whom was himself, and meeting the gods, standing by their sides, becoming—

But he had met a god, to whom he was inconsequential. To everyone, except maybe Bobby, he'd been irrelevant. He had failed, except—

Bobby had made it through.

The knowledge overpowered his jealousy. Helping Bobby on his way had been the purpose Hastur had given him. In that, he had succeeded. He felt glad. Success in service...

He could accept a reduced destiny and adapt to serving one master.

Sheldon was almost to the picnic blanket when Max looked up from the strange but happy foursome and said, "Sheldon!"

Sheldon stopped, a little surprised that Max remembered his name.

"Don't be surprised," Max said. "You and I are on the same team. Come on, sit down, have a drink, have some food."

Sheldon thought of Nick and thought of Bobby, and though Max was cute, he didn't think Max was on the same team in *that* way. "Thank you," he said, and he sat between Max and Steven. The group of five didn't quite form a circle. Janet and Gordon were at the ends of a horseshoe in which everyone had a view of the water.

Janet extended a hand to him. "I don't think we've met," she said. "I'm Janet."

Sheldon shook her hand. "Sheldon," he said. He didn't want to say he knew her name already because he might have to admit that he'd seen her die. She offered him grapes.

The creek's babbling filled the silence while they all ate. Janet shared the grapes with Sheldon while Max crunched on chips. The Marks boys ate sandwiches. Steven's was almost too big for his mouth. Everyone, including young Steven, drank the spiked lemonade. Sheldon quickly concluded that the dead could get drunk.

After a while, Sheldon said, "You all know... I mean I... do you know... you know, don't you... or think..."

"Spit it out, Shel," Gordon said, chewing.

Gordon Marks, the notorious murderer, had called him *Shel*. "Bobby and Heather," Sheldon said. "You know they made it?"

"We know, more or less," Max said. "They made it through the Glass Citadel. Continuing to the Walled City. The Palace."

"I wonder what it's like," Janet said.

Sheldon had heard so many whispers. He had wanted to see them, the City and the Palace, and the voices telling him to stay away had been... irritating. Ignorable. He had been foolish. Hubristic.

Ghosts have more to lose than they know.

"I hope none of us finds out," Max said.

"I want to see it," Gordon said. "What could... Hastur... have on Adam?"

Sheldon laughed, dismissing Gordon's comment as the naiveté of the underread. His thought about ghosts having more to lose lingered, and he realized: he was a ghost, Max was a ghost, Janet was a ghost—

"This is a gathering ground," Sheldon said. "We're a gathering of ghosts."

"You're dead, too?" Janet asked.

"I'm not dead," Steven said.

"What's the significance?" Max asked.

"Bobby and I met... someone... in Lost Carcosa... who talked about gathering ghosts. A challenger who would make way for the organization of... an Army of Ghosts," Sheldon said.

"The Man in the Grinning Mask could have been the challenger," Max said.

"I can accept being a ghost," Janet said, "but I'm not joining any army."

"Everyone in The Middle Reaches serves someone," Max said.

"Maybe we don't have to join," Sheldon said. "Maybe we're here because we're already part of it."

Gordon spoke sharply: "Like my brother said, we're not dead, and *we're* here. I don't know how we're not hurt anymore, but we never died."

"Okay," Sheldon said, and words appeared in his head: "but that doesn't stop you from being parts of the timeless clockwork."

Gordon looked pale.

Sheldon looked at the creek. It only flowed in one direction.

Max

The Herald of The Man had said little enough to seem superfluous, but she had mentioned an army coming in The Man's wake—an Army of Ghosts?

No alarms. No surprises.

Max gazed at the rushing water of Sweetwater Creek, and he looked past it, across, toward the trees, and he saw, standing in a conglomeration of dark hues, The Shadow Man. In service to Hastur and in death, The Shadow Man was Max's reflection. They were both obedient ghosts.

But they were ghosts of different kinds. The Shadow Man did not look like Nick, the revenant at his core, but like an inkblot dreaming of being human. Max followed paths through time and space that didn't always make sense but were for the most part linear, whereas The Shadow Man moved from rift to rift, appearing on others' paths intermittently to beckon or intervene when he—or his master—ordained.

Max could be a conduit for Hastur. The Shadow Man had raw, innate power. If he defected, if he joined an Army of Ghosts, he could be a general, fearsome with what he could drown in his cold well of sadness.

The Shadow Man, Nick, loved Sheldon. Max didn't love anyone anymore.

Max waved at the dark figure, which did not move.

No alarms and no surprises, please.

Sheldon

Sheldon looked where Max waved, and he saw The Shadow Man, Nick, a dark smear collecting more darkness into a hint of a human form, the boy who had loved him and turned into a man who had loved him and died for him and made him feel important.

How could Nick have been so stupid? Sheldon was... unworthy. Why couldn't he have helped Nick the way he'd helped Bobby? Why was Nick a sacrifice turned into the dark figure they'd seen in The Middle Reaches again and again before The Watcher had assessed Sheldon as unfit?

Sheldon's heart pounded, pushing yearning through his veins and arteries. He wanted Nick back. He wanted a second chance. But he knew better than to want things.

He also knew Nick's destiny was higher than watching Sheldon and the monsters' picnic. He closed his eyes and thought, *Go on. Hurry.*

When he opened his eyes, The Shadow Man was gone.

End of *Cycle Two: A Rift in Time and Space*

NEXT IN THIS SERIES

In *The Middle Reaches, Cycle Three: The Flood*, new travelers collide with some familiar from earlier cycles as they all journey deeper into the horrors of Carcosa, exploring the roads to Lake Hali and the Palace of the King in Yellow. A lawsuit in the earthly realm over the ownership of the land between the two Acton Ways, the entryway to The Middle Reaches, manifests in Carcosa as a struggle among gods and ghosts, a struggle that could unleash an apocalyptic Flood.

ABOUT THE AUTHOR

L. Andrew Cooper

L. Andrew Cooper specializes in the provocative, scary, and strange. Other works include book-length stories Alex's Escape, Noir Falling, Records of the Hightower Massacre [with Maeva Wunn], Crazy Time, Burning the Middle Ground,  and Descending Lines; short story collections Leaping at Thorns, Peritoneum, and Stains of Atrocity; poetry collection The Great Sonnet Plot of Anton Tick; non-fiction Gothic Realities and Dario Argento; co-edited fiction anthologies Imagination Reimagined and Reel Dark; and the co-edited textbook Monsters. He has also written 35 award-winning screenplays. After studying literature and film at Harvard and Princeton, he used his Ph.D. to teach about favorite topics from coast to coast in the United States. He now focuses on writing and lives with his husband in North Hollywood, California. Find him at http://landrewcooper.com